The Isis Command
A Barry Ross International Mystery

by Ann Livesay

Silver River Books
Medford ○ Boise ○ London

This Silver River Book contains
the complete text of the original novel.

THE ISIS COMMAND

A Barry Ross International Mystery

First Edition March 1998
All Rights Reserved.

For information address:
Silver River, Inc., 1619 Meadowview Drive, Medford, OR 97504, USA.
The Silver River web site address is http://www.silverriver.com

Library of Congress Catalog Card Number: 98-90067

ISBN 0-9662817-0-5

PRINTED IN THE UNITED STATES OF AMERICA
10 9 8 7 6 5 4 3 2 1

BOOKS BY ANN and MYRON SUTTON

Eastern Forests: An Audubon Society Nature Guide
The Audubon Society Book of Trees
Wildlife of the Forests
The Wild Shores of North America
The Pacific Crest Trail: Escape to the Wilderness
Wilderness Areas of North America
The Wild Places: A Photographic Celebration of Unspoiled America
Yellowstone: A Century of the Wilderness Idea
The Secret Places: Wonders of Scenic America
The Wilderness World of the Grand Canyon
New Worlds for Wildlife
The American West: A Natural History
The Appalachian Trail: Wilderness on the Doorstep
Among the Maya Ruins: The Story of John Lloyd Stephens and
                              Frederick Catherwood
The Life of the Desert
Animals on the Move
Journey Into Ice: Sir John Franklin and the Northwest Passage
Guarding the Treasured Lands
Exploring with the Bartrams
Nature on the Rampage
Steller of the North

INTERNATIONAL EDITIONS

The Audubon Society Book of Trees (Japanese)
Le Monde des Arbes
Walder
Bomen uit de Gehele Wereld
Wildlife of the Forests (Japanese)
Knaurs Tierleben im Wald
Animaux des Forêts
Dierenleven in de Bossen
I Maya
Tiere Unterwegs
Hur Flyttar Djuren?
The Endless Quest
Irrfahrt im Beringmeer

Also in this Series (in preparation):

Death in the Amazon
The Madman of Mount Everest
The Chala Project: Murder in the Grand Canyon
The Dinkum Deaths: Murder on the Great Barrier Reef
Murder in The Alhambra
Barry Ross and the Tiger Bone Gang
Murder at Angel Falls
Murder in the Galápagos
Death Among the Gauchos
Murder in Yosemite

Who is this lord of terror?

Egyptian Book of the Dead

ONE

The night the mummy fell through Maybelle Cartwright's door, she hosted the liveliest party of the year. The Swains fighting and hurling plates. Hami cursing. Molly slicing the air with her finger. Fawzi bent on murder. Mei Hua cringing. A typical night of Turki-bashing.

Lively also, it seemed, because I had arrived in Cairo. I make no bones about it, modest as I am. Wherever I go, there are those who bow in honor, swoon because they think I look like Bogey, fill with curiosity, or get very nervous. My reputation precedes me. I want it to. I want them, meaning the bad guys, to get nervous. That way I could tell them apart. I had no idea what I would run into tonight.

I didn't expect bad guys at Maybelle's. But I would scan everybody just the same to see if I could find the person, or persons, I was looking for. At the least, I might get some leads.

When Maybelle and the Admiral bought this big house overlooking the Nile, it seemed as though he would remain with the Mediterranean Fleet forever. After his death, she stayed on, loving as she did the views of Cairo and the Nile from the veranda, and the long curving driveway overhung with fig and bamboo—her "tunnel entrance," she called it.

And, of course, all those—how shall we call them?—strange, lovable, oddball, brilliant scientists who drove up it for the monthly meeting of the Society. The projects she sponsored, the support she gave to other antiquities research, all endeared her to the Egyptian government. They'd told me so.

That was one of the reasons I had so much respect for Maybelle. No one else I knew gave so much support to saving what was left of the treasures of Egypt. This endeared her to everybody.

I went in, unashamed of my Levis. I knew how archeologists dress at soirées like this, though I did put my baseball cap in my back pocket. If this revealed a receding hairline, I didn't care. They had to take what they got.

This night, particularly, Maybelle gushed about introducing me, nephew of her old New York friend, Kelly Ross, to all the guests. She still couldn't quite understand why Kelly had sent me to Cairo.

"She's always sending me somewhere," I responded, meaning nothing.

"I know that. But why here?" She didn't wait for an answer she doubted would come. "Did Kelly ever tell you about our contest?"

"No."

"When we were at Bryn Mawr, she challenged me to become richer than she."

"Who won?"

"I conceded early. I only got filthy rich. She became super rich."

I smiled. "Now she's spending her fortune as fast as she can."

"We've talked about that. She's trying to clean up the world, save endangered species, habitats... all that."

"I can't keep up with her."

"Bosh!" Maybelle cuffed me on the shoulder. "I happen to know better. You chase criminals from the jungles of the Amazon to the high peaks at Mount Everest. Well, anyway, I can only afford to save Egyptian antiquities."

I looked around the room. "That's why all these people are here?"

"They're archeologists, most of them. Like family to me. They work on different projects, scattered up and down the Nile. But don't be surprised. They're a stubborn and competitive lot. Opinionated. Defensive. Maybe that's what makes them good in their fields. Combative. I just wanted to alert you. They're always fighting each other. Come..."

She led the way to a voluptuous, auburn-haired siren whose black eyes seemed to mask a volcano within. I tried to hold my eyebrow steady so as not to reveal my astonishment. I don't think I've ever seen such a magnificent femme fatale, and my work takes me among the best of the world. She must be a consort of James Bond.

Maybelle touched her arm affectionately. "I want you to meet Andrea Zaragoza."

Or she could be Miss Morocco, Miss Spain, Miss World. She held my hand a trifle longer than protocol required, and looked straight into my eyes longer than necessary... Establishing a connection, I felt...

"I'm Barry Ross," I said, though I knew she knew.

"Yes," she returned. "Maybelle's told us all about you."

"All?"

"All she knows. She hasn't told us why you're here."

I gave her a touch of a wicked smile. "She doesn't know."

"Do you?"

"Let us say I came for the waters."

The corner of her mouth betrayed a smile in response. "You and Rick? This is not Casablanca. I don't believe it. What waters?"

"The Nile, perhaps?"

"Nobody comes for the Nile..." She turned to Maybelle. "He's evading all my questions."

Maybelle went on: "Andrea keeps our operations going. Never had a better accountant or secretary. But I warn you, Barry, she's a hot-headed Spaniard. She's a living answer to the question of what young women in Cairo do for entertainment. They pass out keys to their apartments."

Andrea stiffened in mock resentment. "Maybelle! You embarrass me."

"Nonsense, my dear. Barry must know, if he doesn't already, that Cairo seethes with sex."

I laughed at this, too loudly I think, and said: "Do you know any city that doesn't?"

"Barry!" Maybelle replied. "You are wicked. Actually, I do know one. I spent some time in Punxatawney, Mississippi, when I was young. Didn't get a single offer."

"Oh, Maybelle," I said sadly, "there's no accounting for bad taste."

She squeezed me. "Barry, you're sweet. But come along. I must get you out of Andrea's clutches while I can. I have others for you to meet."

I lingered a moment, trying to look at Miss Spain as tenderly as I could. My blue eyes treatment usually melted them down. "Will I see you again?"

Her face remained a mask. "You'll have to," she murmured in a sultry voice, "if you want the key..."

"See what I mean?" Maybelle said, tugging my arm.

Andrea said: "Is your room satisfactory?"

"Quite, thank you."

"Maybelle suggested Heliopolis, but Della..."

She paused, fishing for information. I filled her in. "Della's my secretary in Washington."

"What company?" Andrea was thorough, I had to say that for her.

I smiled and answered: "Oh, she's very good company."

A trace of anger flashed briefly in Miss Spain's black eyes. Then her lips parted in a faint smile. "Della asked for a modest hotel. I reserved the best I could find."

I thanked her and told her the room looked just fine. She walked away. I bowed and turned to Maybelle, who said: "Follow me, Barry. Let' see who's fighting whom."

She wasn't kidding. She ushered me through the crowded, smoky, bourbon-scented room. A noisy room. Everyone seemed to be arguing at an elevated temperature.

A trio of musicians over by the palms tried to make its Haydn heard—without much success.

Maybelle's ample bulk and rose-flowered dress made her presence commanding. Everybody stopped scowling to hug her as she passed, or at least to look at her with grateful eyes. Later on, the schedule called for each to say a few words about the research done this month under her sponsorship.

Tab and Veronica Swain jested that they had come only for the... "What do you call these tidbits?" Veronica asked, holding up a pasta-covered meat ball. "They're terrific."

"Chicken shumais," Maybelle answered. "Junji's specialty."

"Really? What's in 'em?"

"It's his secret. Meat, pasta, spices. He won't tell me."

"You'd better hang on to Junji. Good Japanese cooks are rare in Cairo."

Maybelle glanced at the bottles on the wet bar. "Empty already?"

"Archeologists are always thirsty," Tab explained.

Maybelle leaned to me. "These people drink so much bourbon, wine and Coke I accuse them of making up for weeks in the desert... They're like shrunken sponges swelling up again. Barry, these are the Swains, Tab and Veronica. This is Dr. Barry Ross—we call him Barry. Get acquainted. I'll be right back." She stepped over to the bar to replenish supplies.

I scanned the Swains—Tab lanky, tall and bearded, Veronica blue eyed, tall and blonde. Her upswept hair was held in place by a jeweled comb. From there on down she was festooned with jewelry, including an armful of bracelets.

I kissed her hand. "What marvelous taste you have in jewelry," I said, using a line that always worked.

"Oh, Dr. Ross," she responded. "You are my friend for life." She turned to Tab in a huff. "You see. Some one appreciates my good taste."

The man replied: "He doesn't know you yet."

"Oh you bastard." She turned away.

I had to look up at them. But then, I'd always said that it was better to be short, tough and wiry instead of tall, thin and wobbly. Each wore a long, flowing caftan, hers a vibrant crimson, his white with vertical stripes that fell from shoulders to floor. Both oozed antagonism toward each other.

"Veronica's from the South," Tab said. "You'll have to overlook her crude behavior."

"*Crude!*" she shouted, lifting a fist.

I interrupted. "What part of the South? I love the South."

She melted. "Barry, you're a dahlin'. Would you marry me?"

"What are you arguing about now?" Maybelle asked, coming back from the bar. Then she said to me quickly, in order to slow their arguing: "The Swains work on Egyptian history before the pharaohs."

"*Before* the pharaohs? Is there any?" I asked the questions mostly to stimulate conversation. It caused a blast.

Veronica drew herself up. "*Is* there any? My god! Listen to that! *Listen* to this guy! *Is there any!* Hah, Doctor, I inform you right now. More fascinating than the pharaohs. You wouldn't believe it."

"I don't."

"What they mean," Maybelle interrupted, "is that they are more fascinated by pre-pharaonic Egypt than the rest of us."

"Well, there's more of it," Veronica responded defensively. "The ancient Egypt most people know goes back only a mere five thousand years. The real history of Egypt goes back *seven hundred thousand years*. It's true!"

"You can't mean it?" I commented, dragging her on.

"I do! Those early people were tough and brilliant. My god, they had to suffer the violence of Nile floods, wild animals, heat. Where do you think the pharaohs got their genes? Where do you think the dynasties first sprang up?" She reflected a moment, then added, with a contemptuous sneer: "Turki doesn't give a shit."

Maybelle explained to me. "Turki's their nemesis. All of them."

"Who's Turki?" I asked.

"I'll answer that," Tab interrupted. "He's the dumbest archeologist the Egyptian government has ever hired."

"Dumb?"

"Well, stupid. They put him in charge of research. That means he has to approve anything anyone proposes in antiquities research. Including Maybelle's projects. Everything. We have to get Turki Husseini's approval for this. Turki Husseini's agreement on that. He's playing a god."

"Why not?" I asked. "Rameses did. How does that make him stupid?"

Veronica burst out: "Turki is no Rameses. Good lord! Rameses was smart."

Maybelle tried to soothe them. "The government's understandably cautious, my dear."

"Of course," Tab barked, waving his arm. "Egypt's a rape victim. Has been for thousands of years. Turki's oversensitive. I know that. I don't blame him. But all he can think of is tombs, tombs, tombs."

I asked blithely: "What else is there?"

"*Listen to that!*" Veronica snapped. "There were obelisks and statues of granite, jewels and boxes made of stuff like gold, alabaster, faience. Gorgeous beyond anything. Hell with that, they're all gone now..."

Tab: "How do you know that?"

"Shut up! Barry, you come out to where we're digging. We'll show you."

"I'd like to, believe me. But I'm afraid..."

Maybelle inserted: "Barry's very busy, my dear. He does investigations on an international scale."

Veronica scowled again. "Then when you see Turki Husseini will you kindly remind him that there's more to Egypt than tombs? Remind him that we're alive?"

Maybelle took my arm and steered me away before this got any worse. "That's my job," she called over her shoulder to Veronica. Then to me, more softly: "They're a hard-

working couple. But Turki does irritate them. I warned them
it wouldn't be easy. He provokes them to fight with each
other."

"Fight?"

"Tab accuses Veronica of bedding down with Turki,
just to get favors. Then Veronica accuses *Tab* of bedding
down with Turki."

I recoiled. "What kind of a mob is this?"

Maybelle laughed. "Mob's the word... You'll see... But
out of this chaos, good science rises. You'll discover that.
Here, I want you to meet Ali Fawzi."

I shook hands with the short, dark Egyptian with the
droll countenance. Fawzi seemed to be listless, drained of
energy, down and out. He exhibited no spirit of enthusiasm
whatever, no welcome to his country, not even word of greet-
ing. He mumbled a word or two, managed a weak smile,
then let his eyes fall to the floor. I looked at Maybelle with
an inquiring expression.

"Ali's in the dumps," she said.

"I can see that," I said.

A look betraying silent fury crossed the Egyptian's face.
"Who wouldn't be?" he snapped.

Maybelle nodded. "Ali's been working his heart out to
find an ancient Egyptian road."

"A road?" I asked: "They *had* a road. They've *always*
had a road. The river, longest in the world..."

"Yes, we know. They used the Nile as a highway. Canoes. Barges. Rafts. But Ali was convinced that they hauled
limestone for the pyramids and granite for the statues over
real, honest-to-goodness *roads*."

"*Any* kind of road," Ali snarled "Even short ones." Then
he frowned. "I looked and looked. No record. None!"

Maybelle sighed. "Sounds silly, doesn't it. The Incas
had roads. The Mayas had roads. Not the Egyptians. None
was ever found, but that didn't stop Ali. He looked and
dug and looked. Nothing."

I tried to commiserate. "The fruits of archeology?"

"No!" Ali looked up as he spoke. His lips curled into a snarl. "I was betrayed."

It was the last word I expected to hear around here. "Betrayed?"

"Yes, I think you say 'double crossed.'"

"By whom?"

"That insect. That snake. Turki. May Allah curse his soul and banish him to the driest desert in the universe. He didn't *tell* me!"

All I could get was anger, with no explanation. "You speak in riddles. Tell you what?"

"That a *German* team was also looking for roads. Out in the desert. Then... Then..." Fawzi became more enraged, incoherent...

Maybelle finished for him. "What he's trying to tell you, Barry, is that last week the Germans announced that they *had* discovered a road. The first time ever in Egypt."

"Turki hates me," Ali burst out. "I *know* he does."

Maybelle tried to calm him. "No, Ali. Surely not..."

"He does! I knew he would betray me some day. I will get even."

"He's just busy. So many other things..."

"He *betrayed* me! I will *kill* him for that. All the hard work! All the time I wasted. Just wasted. I'll kill him. I will."

He became so overwrought he could not go on. He turned abruptly, seething with fury, and left the room.

TWO

Maybelle watched him go, shaking her head.

I said: "He doesn't take it very well."

"The Egyptians," she offered, "work so hard. They cannot afford to waste time. They do not forgive easily."

"You're going to have trouble with that one."

"I have trouble with all of them. I've tried to tell Turki to be more supportive, but sometimes I think he lives on another planet."

A crash and clatter of broken glass issued from the kitchen. Maybelle swerved and made her way there. I followed.

Veronica, holding a plate in a menacing gesture, shrieked at Tab: *"You're a liar! Not a word of that is true!"*

She threw the plate, which missed Tab by a wide margin, and clattered to the tile floor. Junji, the Japanese cook, leaped over and hugged the pile of plates so that Veronica could not get at another.

"Sorry, Junji. Awfully sorry. But that bastard...". She turned toward Tab. They fled from the room.

Maybelle surveyed the damage and sighed. "It's nothing. They're good archeologists. Really."

She looked across the counter to a young, frightened Chinese woman, cowering in dismay. "Ah, Mei Hua," said

Maybelle. "Never mind. I think the worst is over. Come. I want you to meet Barry Ross. Barry, Mei Hua is doing research on color in the temples, what little remains. She's concentrating on the buildings at Kom Ombo and Medinet Habu."

As Mei Hua came forward, I offered my hand and said: "Ni hao. Ni shenti hen hao ma?"

"Hao. Xie xie nin." Her eyes widened with surprise: "Nin shuo putonghua?"

"Wo shuo yidiar Zhongguo hua. Dou bu hao. Ni shi zai char?"

"Ni Zhongguo hua hen hao. Oh, bu shi. Wo shi Jinan ren. Shandong. Ni ne?"

"Mei Guo. Los Angeles. Wo you hen duo de Zhongguo pengyou. Zhongguo ren hen haode ren. Zhongguo hen piao liang, hen you yise, shi bu shi?"

"Shi de. Xie xie nin..."

Maybelle recovered from her astonishment. "Barry, I completely forgot that you speak Chinese. What was that all about?"

"Nothing, really. I asked her how she was; she's surprised that I speak putonghua."

"What's that?"

"National language of the People's Republic. I just told her I have many Chinese friends."

We conversed a bit further in Chinese. Then I said to Maybelle: "She's very polite, but I sense that Turki Husseini doesn't think her work is very important, either."

"He vacillates," Maybelle explained. "One day he feels one way, the next day another."

"She says he disapproved of her project at the beginning."

"Not exactly. He just took his time, delayed her for no apparent reason."

"The Chinese are sensitive about such things," I said. "But very patient."

"And hard-working. She's a charmer, one of our best. Finding a lot about the sources of the coloration on the temples and mortuary places..."

"Turki doesn't think that important?"

"He's brusque, Barry. Turki means well. He's very possessive about Egypt's antiquities. Doesn't want anyone to touch *anything*."

Mei Hua spoke softly. "I understand."

"Of course, you do, my dear," said Maybelle.

As Maybelle led the way out of the kitchen, I said "Zai jian, zai jian," to Mei Hua. I didn't think this Turki Husseini was treating these people very nicely, and said so to Maybelle. She responded that he's very intolerant of sloppy archeologists.

"Are these people sloppy?" I shouldn't have asked it.

"Oh, my no," Maybelle became defensive. "They are among the best. Do you think I would support them if they weren't?"

I changed the subject: "This Turki Husseini sounds very interesting. When can I meet him? Is he here?"

"He's gone. Disappeared somewhere. I haven't heard from him in two weeks. That's all right. He gets involved. He usually attends these meetings. Even though he gets chewed up by these people."

"One of these days he's going to be murdered by one of them. They all hate him?"

"All except Sandy." She beckoned a red-headed, freckle-faced, barrel-chested young scholar to them. As he approached, I tagged him as different from the rest... super serious, no nonsense, highly dedicated.

Maybelle introduced him. "This is Sanford Santano. Everybody calls him Sandy. He is doing what Turki thinks is the most important work of all."

I nodded to Sandy, shook hands. "Tell me about it."

Sandy spoke in a gentle tenor voice. "Well, the engravings and paintings down inside a lot of the tombs and temples are deteriorating, and I got it in mind to record everything once and for all, digitally."

I expressed surprise. "This hasn't been done already?"

"Yes and no," Sandy answered. "J. G. Wilkinson, the Englishman, painted copies of the art work starting in 1821. A good record. The *only* record we have now, because some of the original art work in the tombs has been destroyed. But his paintings can also fade. Copies don't last much either. I want to do the whole thing on disk. Convert it all to digital."

"On photo discs?"

"A lot of it, yes. Then you can make exact copies. Send them as attachments on e-mail. Fax them all over the world. Store them forever. They're numerical. Won't fade or deteriorate."

Maybelle: "We are very lucky to get Sandy to our meetings. He doesn't like to leave his work."

"There isn't much time," Sandy responded.

I asked: "That serious?"

Maybelle: "What he means is that there is so much to be done. He has a team. And lots of equipment. And they work fast. But Sandy's so meticulous, so determined to get it all right..."

Sandy scowled. "Time and human stupidity... We're losing some things before I can get to them."

This astonished me. "Really? How so?"

Maybelle steered me away. "In answer to that question, you must talk to Hami. That's what we call him. His real name is Hasmukhlal Gandhi. He's one of the stalwarts of our group."

She strode to the dark-faced Indian, dressed formally in a white turban. "Dr. Gandhi, this is Dr. Ross."

My first impression was one of respect. Those dark eyes seemed to indicate that he had just come down from a mountain where he sat and dispensed the wisdom of the ages. The Indian's dark eyes lighted.

"Ah, yes, but I've heard of you. My friends in the tiger sanctuaries tell the story of how you captured the Tiger Bone Gang. You are a legend in my country, Dr. Ross."

"Barry, please."

"Barry... But I thought your field was biology."

"It is."

"Then what brings you to Cairo? There's no biology here."

"Oh, there's a little..."

Maybelle responded to the question. "He goes wherever his Aunt Kelly sends him."

Hami turned to her. "Ah, but Maybelle, this man is very famous in India."

"He's famous everywhere," she said.

"Yes," Hami went on, "but some of my countrymen are so stupid and this man stopped them from selling tiger bone powders. Stopped them when we couldn't. I am honored..."

Maybelle put her arm in Gandhi's. "You yourself are one of our favorites, Hami. We've just been telling Barry what everyone does. He's surprised that so many have a grudge against Turki."

His black eyes flared. "That bastard!"

I was jolted again by the sudden venom. I wasn't exactly prepared for all this in a group of scholars.

"Excuse my language," Gandhi went on. "I really don't see how *anything* gets done around here with that man in charge."

Maybelle: "He likes your work."

"Then why doesn't he let me do it?"

I held up a hand and shook my head in confusion. "What are you talking about?"

Gandhi's voice remained controlled, but with effort. "Archeologists for years have come in and dug and taken out fabulous treasures...then just walked away. Left things in ruin."

"Under Egyptian supervision?"

"No. English. French. In the Valley of the Kings at Thebes, they opened up tombs, let in moisture. That did it."

I frowned in disbelief. "There's moisture out there? I've always found Egypt dry as a bone."'

ⓦⓦⓦⓦⓦⓦⓦⓦⓦⓦⓦⓦⓦⓦⓦⓦⓦⓦⓦⓦⓦⓦⓦⓦⓦⓦⓦⓦⓦⓦⓦⓦ

"From the few rains that come. Result is that the floors and walls are cracking. Paintings flaking off. You should see the tomb of Seti I."

"You're serious?"

"You wouldn't want to see Tut's tomb... After more than three thousand years, modern man opens it and it's deteriorating."

"Everything gone?"

"No, praise Allah. The tomb of Rameses IV still has some fantastic wall paintings..."

"What's being done about it?"

Maybelle: "That's where Hami comes in. His project is conservation."

Gandhi: "Cleaning up after the archeologists is a more correct way of saying it. I'm studying the hydrology of the Valley of the Kings—the underground water circulation—so that we can decide what to do."

I didn't quite understand. "Where does Turki fit into that? I'd think he'd approve."

"Guilty as the rest. He follows their line. Research is a form of conservation. I think your American word for that is bullshit. Their research started all this."

Maybelle: "Come now, Hami. Turki does like your work. I've heard him say so. He's behind you."

"Far behind! I never see him. He takes weeks to approve my purchase orders... He scarcely knows I exist."

"Hami, you must be patient with the bureaucracy."

"He's like the others. Find some new tomb. Dig it out. Open up a new treasure. Be famous. Go down in history. Screw up the ruin."

I grinned. "That's a generic lament, Hami, worldwide."

Gandhi: "I'm sorry, Barry. I do hope you have a fine time amongst us. Will you get to Thebes while you're here? Karnak? Luxor?"

"I've seen them all, and anxious to get back."

"I invite you to see what I'm doing."

"I'd like that. Thank you."

Maybelle moved through the crowd, introducing me right and left. At length we came to Molly Holly, a young woman with straight black hair, blue eyes, and a serious look on her face. She was young yet, but I could tell from the look on her face that some day she would be a respected schoolmarm or professor. I asked what she did.

"Logographic aspects of the ancient Egyptian language," she said, matter-of-factly.

"Interesting," I responded. I'd always been interested in early forms of writing, perhaps because they seemed so incomprehensible. "Have you compared them with Sumerian and Chinese? They were all contemporaneous, more or less."

Holly looked surprised. "Why, yes, I have."

"Chinese," I went on, "is logographic. Not alphabetic. The hieroglyphs were alphabetic. Helpful, perhaps. But eventually glyphs fail."

By this time Molly Holly's eyes had opened wide and she stood stock still. "Why?" she asked.

"There are ideas and nuances that a pictographic writing system can't express."

Holly almost stammered. "I... You're the first person I've met here who even begins to know what I'm talking about... I'm..."

"But Turki Husseini must certainly have...?"

"That *blob!*" she sneered.

I laughed and turned to Maybelle. "This is almost unanimous!"

"I told you," Maybelle said. "He's trying to keep them all honest."

"Noble, don't you think?"

"Perhaps. But have you ever known an archeologist who wanted to be kept honest?"

"I see your problem."

"We must talk again," said Molly Holly, still startled. "I need your advice."

I protested that I wasn't an expert, only a student of that subject, and would be glad to learn from her. She smiled, and suggested we get together.

"He'll try," Maybelle inserted, "but I fear he's going to be frightfully busy."

We went on. Maybelle glanced toward the wet bar. "Empty again!

Barry, will you excuse me?"

"Certainly."

"Look around. Introduce yourself to the ones you haven't met. I'll be right back." She left for the kitchen.

THREE

Tired of the din, of meeting new people and hearing more tales of woe, I moved to the edge of the crowd.

Andrea Zaragoza walked toward me. I looked away. I didn't feel ready for her yet. She said nothing, but as she passed, she pressed into my hand a small envelope.

I knew what it held. I could feel the outline of the key. She smiled demurely, as a siren tempting Ulysses. I bowed my head in acknowledgment. She moved away and disappeared among the guests.

I put the key in my pocket.

What was I to make of her? She was one of the few here who didn't have a grudge against Turki Husseini. Not being an archeologist, she probably had little to do with him.

Egyptian artifacts near the door caught my eye. I wandered into the vestibule and examined a small obelisk carved from solid granite. Then a delicate Horus, a hawk-headed god, done in alabaster. And on the wall, a modern painting on papyrus, replicating Egyptian musicians playing flutes and sistra.

How good to be back in Egypt, I thought. *I love this place. No country on earth has such an elegant history. So beautiful. So torn apart... It disappeared after the Christian era had begun.*

Collapsed two centuries before the Muslim Era. I felt a tinge of sadness that the ancient artists and farmers and pharaohs were gone. What I would give to walk among them...

Well, anyway, I felt good being in Cairo, another world, another century... A city that didn't even exist during the great dynasties...

My reflections were interrupted by the chime of the doorbell.

I stepped away from the door so that someone from the household might answer the ring. But loud voices, raised with the aid of bourbon, drowned out the bell.

I waited another moment. No one came.

I waited for a second ring.

It never came.

I looked in vain for Maybelle. For *someone.*

A few more seconds passed. I examined a small statue of Sobek, the crocodile-headed god.

No one had heard the chime. No one would arrive. The caller must still be there. So I would open the door myself.

I grasped the elegant brass handle on the giant paneled wooden door and pulled.

As the door opened, a heavy weight seemed to push inward. I had not expected that. The door slammed against me. Caught off guard, I fell backward.

A large, decorated mummy case plunged into the room with a loud **CRASH!** On striking the waxed wooden panels of the floor, the case broke into two pieces, which slid to the edge of the crowd.

A shriek of surprise, heard above the din. Heads turned. Talk stopped. The guests pressed forward.

I got back on my feet and dashed for the door. No one there. No one in sight outside. Not even a car racing away...

Maybelle pushed through the onlookers and broke free, entering the vestibule.

I came back in and stood above the mummy case. One half of it, the lid, lay to one side, empty. The other contained what appeared to be a human figure wrapped in a light cream-colored cloth, steeped in blood.

Murmurs and muffled screams came from the assemblage as each person pressed forward to see better.

"Where, in the name of Osiris," Maybelle's voice seemed to shake a little, "did this come from?"

I replied: "The door bell rang. Once. I was standing there. When no one came, I answered. As soon as I opened the door, this fell in."

Maybelle looked down. "Must be some kind of joke?"

I answered: "I doubt it." I pointed to the wrappings. "May I?"

Maybelle shook her head. "We must wait for the police."

I said softly. "I have an honorary commission from the department of security. If you will have someone call the police..."

Sandy Santano volunteered: "I will." He turned and made his way through the crowd.

I repeated: "May I?"

Maybelle: "Well, if you... If you think it's all right..."

I raised my voice. "Will everybody witness, please? Spread out and widen the circle."

While they jostled into place, I knelt and began to peel away strips of cloth from the head.

Slowly the dark features of the face, dirty and blood-stained, became visible. Some of the onlookers cringed and turned away.

When the closed eyes and the long nose came into view, several voices whispered at once.

"Turki!"

A hush fell over the guests. No one moved. The music ended. Conversations faded to silence. Clink of glasses stopped.

Maybelle said: "Nothing clears the mind like a corpse in the living room."

I asked, in a slow, deliberate tone: "I take it that this is Turki Husseini."

No one responded at once. No one seemed able to speak. The initial shock spread, consumed them, left them speechless. They looked in disbelief, trying to control their emotions, or letting their emotions loose and gasping in surprise.

Maybelle answered. "*Was* Turki Husseini."

For a few moments, no one said anything. I looked from one to another, studying very carefully the expressions on their faces. I looked for Ali Fawzi, who had said, with such bitterness, that he would murder Turki Husseini. He was not around.

Then Hasmukhlal Gandhi addressed me in a low, sepulchral tone: "*You got here too late.*"

FOUR

I immediately cleared the lobby by asking Maybelle to round up all the guests and write down when and where each had last seen Turki Husseini alive and under what circumstances. I warned all the guests to expect questioning in the next few days and not to leave the country without notifying Security. Maybelle led them into the library.

As soon as the security officer, Omar Samaan, middle-aged, bespectacled, obviously tired and harried, arrived, we turned to the corpse. Sandy Santano stood by as witness, taking digital photos at each stage.

Omar did not seem to have much taste for this. He spoke English passably and complained that he had been involved in a multiple murder case and was just about to leave for the south of Egypt. Short, light-complected for an Egyptian, he felt relieved when he learned who I was. That was ominous. I deferred to him in what followed, so that he wouldn't get any ideas that I might want to take over. Turki was Egyptian. Omar had to take charge, and he knew it. But even though he said he had known Turki, his heart didn't seem to be in this otherwise routine work. I couldn't determine why, beyond his statement that he was on another case.

We took the corpse out of the mummy case, laid it on a sheet, and unwrapped it. Beneath the shrouds, Husseini was entirely naked, though he had what you might call a coat of blood. He had bled profusely, the red turned dark and congealed in the body hair, ears, eyes, everywhere. For a while, the source of bleeding, if there was a wound, eluded us.

Judging from the condition of the flesh, the state of the dried blood, the rigidity of the limbs, I fixed the time of death at about six hours earlier. A guess at best. There did not seem to be any signs of poison, although we couldn't be sure without lab tests. We did detect a stench of alcohol, which meant that Turki may have been drugged with the stuff against his will. Liquor is taboo here, and I assumed that Turki, if he were a devout Muslim, did not imbibe. It was hard to ignore the possibility, though, that he could have been forced to drink, then passed out. If so, he might have been immobilized when death occurred.

It seemed improbable that liquor had been the cause of death, however, except in the sense that it veiled his vision and made him vulnerable to murder. Internal convulsions might have led to discharge of blood, but they would have to be caused by something more than whiskey, even bad whiskey. He had apparently coughed up blood, but that could have been from the lungs. Thinking that the lungs might have been punctured, I went back to a more thorough examination of the skin, particularly around the torso.

By scraping away the crust of blood—which I now began to think had been deliberately smeared over the body, as though in some satanic ritual—I could get a better view of possible puncture points. Turki had hair on his back, and a lot of it, which hampered the search. By pushing the flesh, pinching minutely, and going at it one square inch after another, I finally found a small slit about twelve millimeters wide. Probing this, seeing how deeply it went, I concluded that he had been stabbed in the back by some kind of stiletto, small saber, scissors, or letter opener. Whatever the weapon, it had gone deeply and probably punctured a lung.

I searched for other punctures but could find only the one. Omar finished his on-the-scene staff work, examining the mouth and teeth, ears, chest, stomach, genitals, anus, legs and feet. He seemed to do a thorough job, and I respected him for it. When he was done, we tentatively agreed that the only conclusion at the moment was that Turki had been stabbed in the back.

By the time we finished, it was nearly midnight. The other guests had gone. Maybelle invited Sandy to stay in one of the spare bedrooms for the night. As he left the living room, I said to her: "You really put on quite a party."

"Oh, Barry, I'm frightfully distressed by all this. And I'm furious! Someone is intent on humiliating me, right in front of my guests."

I took her hand and held it affectionately. "Maybelle, I can't believe that Turki was killed just to embarrass you. But whoever did this had a sense of drama."

"Barry, be careful. Now that everybody knows who you are and what you do, watch yourself. When someone as famous as you comes to Cairo, the underworld gets nervous. Whoever did this could want you out of the way before you find out who."

I said quickly: "It's not my job to find out anything about this."

"Barry, you're already in the midst of this, and you are a crime investigator, and you've inherited some of this by default. You could be the next target."

"I usually am, Maybelle. Let me worry about that. Perhaps I will see you tomorrow."

"I hope so, Barry."

Omar offered to drive me to my hotel. On the way out toward Giza, he didn't say much. Then he turned to me and became very frank.

"Barry, I can't do this."

"What do you mean?"

"I have terrorist plots, Satan worshipers, and revolutions. Little revolutions. Yes. Too much. All of it. Too much. How can I do wild bunch of archeologists?"

I defended Maybelle's mob. "They're not wild. Believe it or not, Omar, they're well-trained and disciplined."

He replied: "Barry, I not able to do this. Too much. Too much."

I shut up, stifled an answer, hoped this whole conversation would go away.

"We need you. Very badly."

"I'm here on another case, Omar."

"Well, of course, I suppose you are. You have many cases. That is why we need you."

"Meaning...?"

"You so famous. Very famous. Known all over world. Egyptian government appreciate it if, please, you would—."

I cut in immediately. "Omar, Turki Husseini was an employee of the Egyptian government. I'm here on other business."

"Yes. Yes, of course. I know. But all those Americans, all those people at the Cartwright house, they are suspects. You can handle them better than anyone in my country. I have no one in all Egypt to help. No one. You listen. Who has skills you have? You could put this in under tent, maybe, yes? Maybe this help your other business. Good eh?"

"Possible. But—." I stopped. I didn't want to argue. I didn't want to agree, and tried not to think of it. But there was only one inescapable conclusion. He was right. Right as hell. I didn't like it. Didn't like getting snookered into this in such a way. Yet there was the handwriting on the wall as plain as an Egyptian hieroglyph.

I was getting caught squarely in a trap that was not of my own making. If I screwed up tonight, made him mad just to get him off my back, where would that get me? What would happen tomorrow and the next day and the next when I might need his help on my own project? *Don't be stupid, Ross. You could wind up needing this guy on your side.*

"Barry, I tell you we are desperate," Omar said. "I help you on both jobs. Call on me. Trust me. But I have no, as you say, point man to work on this case. All Egypt will thank you very, very much if you find out who killed Turki."

We entered a glittering avenue of cabarets with beck-
oning signs—MOHAMED'S RETREAT—CHEZ ALI—
AHMED'S POOL ROOM—. Omar stopped in front of the
most glittering—CRAZY HORSE SALOON. "How about
a show?"

I looked at my watch. "Now?"

"Sure. You like girls? Belly dancing?"

"Of course, I like girls. But, Omar, it's after midnight."

"We'll be out at three. A gift to you. What you think?"

I knew exactly what was happening. I'd fallen into this
sort of thing before. Omar didn't say so, but he had a bud-
get with which to show VIPs around. He couldn't afford
these clubs by himself but he wanted to see the show. I had
no choice. Omar could be a valuable ally. Diplomacy de-
manded that I yield.

"Good show?" I asked.

He forced a grin. "I think good."

He led the way in.

We emerged at 3:15 a.m., bleary-eyed, faces drawn,
bathed in smoke.

"Good girls, huh?" Mohamed exulted.

I nodded politely. We got in the car and drove to my
hotel, a three-star establishment off the beaten path where
I could have at least a little privacy.

Omar made one last plea. "You will help us?"

I smiled as best I could. "At this hour, Omar, you have
worn me down. I will try to find out about Turki. Do what
I can. But no promises…"

He grabbed my hand. "Oh good, good! No. No. I make
no promises. I understand. Thank you! Thank you! Here's
my card. Call me when you need help. Any help."

"Good night, Omar."

I stood there a moment, watching him drive away, stu-
pidly hoping I could start the last twenty-four hours over.
Knowing what I know now, I would never have gone to
Maybelle's, never gotten tangled with Tab and Veronica and

Ali and Hami and Molly and Mei Hua. Never got caught up in a homicide that was none of my business.

Never's a strong word, you idiot. You might need these guys. All of them.

FIVE

The city at last seemed asleep. Not a soul stirred in the hotel. I got a key from a sleepy attendant at the small desk, and climbed the stairs to the third floor.

Wary, as always, I inserted the key, turned it and opened the door a crack. Putting my hand through, I found the wall switch, turned on the light and peered inside. Nobody visible. But the moment I opened the door a little wider, I knew that someone had entered.

The immediate question was whether that someone still remained hidden in the room...

My mental snapshot of the room as I had left it—bed, night stand, dresser, chair, small coffee table—did not coincide with what I saw now.

I had configured the room before leaving. Briefcase placed on the coffee table in a direct line between two opposite corners of the table. Paperback book left on the dresser with the spine toward the briefcase. Newspaper on the night stand with the corner toward the briefcase. Everything now lay askew.

The briefcase had been realigned toward the bathroom door, the paperback book swivelled toward the back wall, and the newspaper now pointed toward the bed. Someone had examined each of these items, taking care to put them back where they'd been found, but not *exactly* in the same position. A room cleaner might have moved one or two, but most likely not all three. In any case, the warning flag flew in my mind.

I listened. No sound. No movement. I moved cautiously to the briefcase and opened it. Books on Egypt. Chinese lessons. Pens. Note pads. Rubber bands. Paper clips. Portable radio. Nothing missing inside. Nothing valuable missing because I had taken valuables and classified materials in the dilapidated canvas bag to Maybelle's. The bag now hung from my shoulder.

Once more I scanned the room, head and eyes moving like a panning camera. Could there be something I *hadn't* left in the room? Booby trap? Explosives beneath the chair or bed, poison gas, germs, toxic dust, a lethal substitution in the bathroom, a deadly spray instead of deodorant?

Examining the bath room, I saw nothing I hadn't brought. I smelled nothing unusual. Although, at this hour, I acknowledged ruefully to myself, I did not trust my senses.

Testing the toothpaste, I brushed my teeth. After that, I walked slowly back into the main room, switched off the light, disrobed and got into bed. The sagging eyebrows and dulling brain drew me toward oblivion almost before I could adopt a comfortable position...

Suddenly, I heard a faint noise.

My eyes opened again and brain went on alert. My ears had picked up a faint rustling sound. It hadn't been much. A slight noise *within* the room. I strained to listen, becoming aware of the passage of a car outside. The soft sound of a whirring fan somewhere. Then a near silence inside the room. But not quite.

Something in the room moved. Something alive. Something, in fact, under the sheet, in bed with me. I leaped out of the bed like a rocket off a pad, thinking: "I *checked* the bed. The spread had been only slightly ruffled."

In the same movement, I flicked on the lamp, and could see the lump, which I had mistaken for a disheveled spread. A muffled hissing sound, a movement of the sheet. I seized a corner of the sheet and flung it away.

A black cobra, a small one. Not the ten feet of an adult, but lethal just the same, and moving toward me.

I flung the sheet back on the bed, rolled the cobra in it, made a large bag, and tied it with a rubber band from the briefcase.

Picking up Omar's card, I dialed the number. He should be home by now. The voice sounded very sleepy. "Who? Barry?"

"Yes, Omar. I found a cobra in my bed."

"You're dreaming."

"Well, I rolled the dream into one of the bed sheets. I'm piercing the sheet with holes so the dream can breathe. Tomorrow morning, I'd like a biologist, or someone from a snake farm, to come get it. And not kill it. You understand?"

A pause, then: "Yes, sir."

"Could you also have someone find out who rented, or bought, a cobra at whose reptile farm yesterday?"

"I'll try."

"Let me know?"

"Of course. Sleep well, Barry. I'm very sorry..."

"Good night, Omar."

SIX

Omar's boy came and got the cobra early next morning.

While showering, I added things up. I've been here a day. Made zero progress on what I came for. Gotten saddled with a murder I don't want. Become caretaker of a cobra intended to assassinate me. And fallen in with a mob of oddball archeologists intent on murder.

One of them could well be the actual murderer, the way they all talked. Or they could have conspired, combined their anger and resources, hired some help and gotten the guy out of their hair. That was the one thing they all wanted. With vehemence. Get rid of him so they could work. He didn't seem to be helping them much anyway.

All I had to try to find out was who actually did the job and try to get proof.

With this baggage, I'm falling backward already.

I decided it was time to see whether Julie and Joe had arrived, and to brief them on disasters up to now. I had overslept, so I left the hotel, reeling a little, even so, from lack of sleep.

Julie and Joe were both energetic, brilliant, and promising, he a lanky blonde cowboy and wildlife biologist from Wyoming, she a park ranger whose most recent post, before they got married last week, was inner canyon ranger at the Grand Canyon in Arizona. After what we'd just gone through in the Grand Canyon, they were heroes in my book.

I had hired Joe on a trip into the Amazon. I hired Julie just last month. Brilliance is why I'd wanted them on my team. And toughness and fearlessness. They were young, though, and this Cairo business looked like it could age them rapidly.

The taxi crossed over to Roda Island and stopped at the entrance to Club Mediterranée at Manial Palace. At the gate I asked: "Bonjour. Je cherche un G.M. du village."

The guard pointed inside. "L'office, s'il vous plaît. A gauche."

I went to the office, showed my identification card from Egyptian Security, and said: "Je suis ami des G. M. Muck."

The attendant gave me their room number. I went down a street under a dense canopy of fig trees and rapped a couple times on the door. Shortly, a crack appeared, someone inside pulled the door open, I slipped in quietly.

As with most rooms at Club Med villages, this one served only two guests, with small beds—cots, really, but comfortable enough, as I'd found at other clubs—and little space for guests. I sat in the only chair, facing Julie and Joe. The wooden window slats remained shut, so no one could see in or out. A small lamp with a dim yellow light illuminated the room with a soft glow.

After the usual affectionate hugs and embraces, Joe spoke first, kidding as usual. "Make it short. I want to go back to the pool."

Only a week ago I had been riding with them on his ranch along the Sweetwater River in Wyoming. We galloped across the grassy swales and slowed to a trot through forests of lodgepole pine and headed up a ridge behind the corrals.

Both were expert riders. Julie had spent two summers in the Grand Canyon, and riding the trails as a law enforcement officer was not a picnic. She guarded her words (with Joe around, she never got many words in edgewise anyway), and when she spoke you listened because you knew something wise and smart was going to be heard.

Joe had competed in rodeos at Cheyenne and knew how to hang on to a horse, no matter what. I'd never met anyone so ebullient, effervescent, and...well, how many adjectives could I apply to such a good-hearted dynamo?

We'd gone up into the high country, among thick forests of spruce, to an overlook. The river wound from the hills to the right to a cleft in a rim of rock far to the left.

"Smell that!" Joe had said, referring to the clear air touched with the scent of spruce. "Fella, this is God's country!" Then he thought for a moment. "I just wish God would pay the taxes on it..."

They had such a sense of humor. Such joy of living. And boundless energy. I rejoiced at seeing them again. "Seems like the wedding was only yesterday. How've you two been?"

"Breathless," Julie answered. "When you were in Wyoming you told us to have a quick honeymoon."

Joe laughed, and said in mock resentment: "We didn't even get started. Sam Petrie called and wanted us to be in Egypt yesterday."

I offered a solution: "Honeymoon in Cairo?"

Julie: "What's up?"

Joe: "Why all the secrecy?"

I lowered my voice. "I don't want anyone in Cairo to see us together. You're here on a special mission. My job is to track you. Get you into trouble."

Joe grinned. "You're good at that!"

"So last night I'm invited to a party by Maybelle Cartwright, a friend of Aunt Kelly, and without any fanfare, a murder falls into my lap—literally."

Julie: "That sounds like you. What happened?"

I described the night's events, concluding emphatically: "I did not come here to investigate a murder."

Joe: "Don't give us that! You were put on this earth to investigate murders."

Julie added: "And you are paid by Aunt Kelly to dig into—."

I clapped my hands, half in anger. "That's the obvious part of it. This is one time she *didn't* have a murder in mind."

Julie: "Well, then, there'll *be* one."

"There's *been* one," I snapped. "And the Egyptian security people don't have time to solve it."

Joe laughed loudly, then muffled himself. "When Barry Ross is around, the cops never have time to solve anything."

"They've tagged you?" Julie asked.

I dropped my shoulders. "They've tagged me." I spread my hands in a gesture of helplessness. "And if I want any favors from Omar Samaan—or anyone in the Egyptian government—on our *real* project, we had better solve this case pronto."

Joe: "Whaddaya mean *we*? We're not supposed to know you. And what's this about our real mission? We haven't been told anything. We have no mission. Mine is to get back to the pool."

"Last night I had a cobra in my bed..."

Joe jumped on that. "A code name for someone? Who was she? Can I help?"

Julie cuffed him on the ear. "You're married now, cowboy."

I grinned. "A *real* cobra. Someone doesn't want me here."

"So?"

"So I don't know which case I'm not wanted here on."

Joe sighed. "As Captain Goode said in *King Solomon's Mines*, 'you're being confoundedly enigmatic.' Once and for all, what's going on?"

I hesitated a moment, not quite sure I myself could sort out and put together everything that had occurred.

"Okay, here's what we have. I go to a meeting of archeologists and others sponsored by Maybelle Cartwright. Most tell tales of woe regarding a government archeologist named Turki Husseini, who oversees their work. To hear them tell it, he's indifferent, antagonistic, obstructive—in short, we got twenty people with motives. One even said he was going to kill Turki."

Julie's eyes narrowed as she grinned. "Makes your job easy, then?"

I said only "Hah!" then went on. "In the middle of the evening, the object of their disaffection falls through the front door, dead as a mummy. Stabbed. Covered with dried and caked blood."

Julie suggested that that murder and their mission—whatever it might be—could be connected.

I didn't want to believe it, and said so. "I first thought of that as preposterous in a city this large. But, of course, you could damned well be right. Everything in Cairo is connected with everything else. All we have to do is find the answers out there among twenty million people."

Joe said, wrinkling his face in mock despair: "I want to go back to Wyoming."

Julie asked: "You'll have to interview all those archeologists?"

"That is one thing I refuse to do. I don't have the time."

"You'd better *take* time," Joe warned, "if you want anything from the government."

"I'll help the government," I answered, "but not by interrogating every weirdo archeologist in Egypt. I wish you could meet the Swains. You'd see what I mean."

'Who are they?"

"Never mind. I have other plans. We have a time lock on our original mission."

Joe scowled. "Now wait a minute. What kind of time lock? It might help a little if you told us why we're here."

I glanced at my watch. "Samaan's picking me up at noon."

"Then you'd better make a long story short."

SEVEN

"Aunt Kelly is an incurable collector. Collects anything, everything. Buys things one year, gives them away the next. Last week she went down to her favorite agent's shop in Manhattan on nothing more than a routine visit...to see if he'd managed to acquire anything new and tempting...

"She's a top customer, knows antiques thoroughly, has traveled a lot, bought abroad. He can't fool her. They've had a wonderful friendship for many years. They are always kidding each other. Kelly could take it as well as dish it out. I can imagine every word of what happened."

The sign over the door spoke for the owner and the elegance of his merchandise:

Juergen Bigelow, Esquire
Collectibles • Rare Art
Exquisite Keepsakes

Kelly emerges from her limousine, ignores the roar of traffic on Fifth Avenue, and marches inside, a brisk step for a sixty-year-old. Short, straight-backed, with hair an elegant gray clipped in a sharp upsweep that makes her look like a flattop, she commands attention like an approaching velociraptor. Her brown eyes dart in all directions as she passes beneath the silken draperies and enters the main salon. She wears no hat. Around her neck, a string of pearls spills out over a white linen jacket and turquoise Thai silk sheath dress.

Juergen Bigelow emerges from a side room, pencil behind his ear, watch fob dangling from his gray vest, with more the bearing of a college professor grading papers than a dealer approaching his richest customer. He's known Kelly Ross long enough to be able to greet her in shirt sleeves—the ultimate intimacy in this world of Ming vases and Navplion craters.

"Good morning, Kelly." He tries to be cheerful.

She gets down to business, her terse gravel voice suggesting that she wants answers fast. "I'm buying. What do you have this week?"

Bigelow raises his eyes to the ceiling in distress, as usual. "Kelly, your approach to collecting is akin to animal tropisms. You see, you want, you buy. Of course, after reducing my prices to a pauper's wage."

"Juergen," she says, in a tone that Queen Victoria would have reserved for her equerry, "I am the best nest-builder you know. Without me, you would *be* a pauper."

"How can I answer your question, 'What do you have this week?' The only constant I have is that you are fond of orange. That sets you apart as a separate species."

She sniffs. "Juergen, I am not subhuman. I know what I want when I see it."

"Come, come, now. Let's see if we can give this some sort of...I mean, you have the most beautiful quartz sphere in New York. What can I do when you *have* everything already?"

"Oh stop it, Juergen. Fish and ravens collect pebbles. I want something significant..."

"Why? You'll only give it away to a museum in a year or two." He sighs in admiration. "Processing a big tax deduction."

She laughs in a diabolical way. "Yes. Best way I know to foil the tax thieves."

"So is giving to UNESCO to fund your nephew's investigations. How is he, by the way?"

"Barry? Just got out of the Grand Canyon. He's in Wyoming. His assistant is getting married."

"Really? I thought he was up on Mt. Everest somewhere."

"That was last month. Now, Juergen..."

"All right. What do you mean by *significant*."

"You're the expert."

"Okay, if you want something ferocious, I can get you an Assyrian collection."

"No."

"Something noble. Grecian? You have a house full of Greece already."

"Try something else."

"Eloquent simplicity. Chinese? Or, I should say, more Chinese?"

"Have it, too."

"Highly decorative. Persian? You haven't bought anything Persian in a year."

"Possible. What else?"

"There's always the complex symbolism of East Indian..."

"Maybe."

"Exuberance? The Renaissance?"

"I like that. Go on."

"Modern? Intellectualized abstractionism? You haven't liked it, up to now."

"Still don't like it. Look, Juergen, I'm thinking of a soirée for some UN people and their families. What do you have in thematic? Anything in fashion this year?"

"Grace and grandeur are always in fashion. And that's all I have left. Egyptian. If so, I can get you something new and exciting."

This raises her eyebrows. "Yes?"

Bigelow returns to his office and reappears with a four-page folder printed in color.

"This just came on the market," he explains. "Never before offered." He points to the photographs. "A tomb in the time of Amenemhet and Senwosret I. Pale pink alabaster statuette of Mentuhotep. What do you think?"

Kelly's eyes narrow, a sign that she's been hooked. "Go on."

He turns the page. "Figurine in faience. Necklace of hammered gold."

"Same period?"

"Yes, Twelfth Dynasty. These are all from the same tomb, I would guess. This is just an announcement brochure. Samples of the collection."

"How many pieces?"

"Thirty or forty, I think, why?"

"Where are they?"

"In Egypt."

"Who's offering?"

"It's private, Kelly. I'm not at liberty to divulge——."

"What museum?"

"Private, never been offered before."

Kelly stops. That's just the kind of thing that blows her top. She turns over the brochure, her mind six weeks ahead. She bids for time. "I rather like this. But before I decide, let me see what you have in Persian or Turkish decoration."

I know her. That's just stalling. For half an hour in one of the back salons she mulls over what he brings in. She pores over sumptuous pieces, principally turquoise, takes them to the light for examination with a magnifying lens.

Her eyes grow darker as she mulls over the pieces. If I'd been there, I would have known instantly that some-

thing had just singed her brain, and that a storm was brew-
ing, something Juergen couldn't know.

She marches back to the outer parlor to pick up the
Egyptian folder.

"May I keep this?"

"Certainly."

"Well, I like the Persian. But I'd also like to see more
of this."

"Go to Egypt?"

"I have some young cousins. I trust their judgment.
How the devil do they make contact? What do they do?
Whom do they meet when they get there?"

"I myself don't know, Kelly. Call me tomorrow."

Without another word, she turns and leaves.

EIGHT

She pushes her driver to get to the UN building as fast as he can, opens the car door herself, and stalks inside like a panther. She knows right where to go, and when she gets there, she enters and slams the door so hard that all the bric-a-brac on Sam Petrie's shelves—statuettes of olive wood, teak, lava, jade, bone—shake and rattle.

"*Sam!*" The tone and timbre of Kelly's voice says hopping mad.

Sam Petrie, UN special projects officer, has no warning. He seldom does when Kelly bursts in. He's grown accustomed to Kelly's violence. Her selective funding of certain projects gives her entry over anyone. Ordinarily he's calm and collected. Not when she's around. His bald pate, graced with white sideburns, reddens. His eyes take on a gentle look as he tries to deflect the assault.

"Kelly! What a wonderful surprise! Did you get the Indian rug I sent you from the Grand Canyon?"

"Yes. It's lovely and I appreciate it. How much did that cost me?"

"It's the thought that counts," he responds promptly. "Please. Sit down."

"Never mind. Sam, I'm mad as hell."

"I detected that, but I didn't get the door locked in time."

She doesn't laugh. "I've just come from Juergen Bigelow's. He gave me *this*."

She flings the Egyptian folder on Sam's desk with a flourish, too mad to take the chair he offers. Without waiting for him to read it, she bursts out: "Thirty or forty pieces, he tells me. Private. First time offered. Look at them. That's just a sample."

"They seem authentic," Sam says, peering closely at the folder.

"Of course, they're authentic!" She pounds his desk. "Somebody's discovered a tomb and robbed it. When in the billy hell are you going to stop this?"

I can see Sam's eyes rolling toward the ceiling. There was never much you could say in the face of a Kelly onslaught. "Oh, Kelly, the illegal trade of Egyptian antiquities has been going on for three thousand—."

"You condone it because it's always been done?"

"Of course not—."

"Then don't take pains to excuse it."

"Kelly, I merely offer a bit of history."

"History can be changed. It's time to have it stopped."

"How? The Luxor obelisk was given to France by Egypt and set up in the center of the Place de la Concorde in Paris, inspiring every thief from here to Hong Kong."

"Sam—."

"Have you been to the Metropolitan Museum here? Egypt gave us the Temple of Dendur. And Cleopatra's Needle in England? *Two thousand* other museums have these things, a lot of it loot. Egypt is fair game for robbery. I've talked to the curators. I ask them to take it back to Egypt. They look at me like I was crazy."

Kelly's eyes go grim. "I can imagine."

"Like some kind of idiot. The Egyptians gave us the entire temple of Dendur, they say. 'No one's asking for anything back. They couldn't protect it if you gave it back to them.'"

Kelly's face takes on a blacker look than ever. "Do you believe that?"

"No."

"Then it is time to bring this insanity to a halt."

Sam drops his shoulders. "Don't you think I've tried? What would you suggest?"

"Here's a thief, or a gang of thieves, that somehow discovered—or broke into—a tomb. Or else, they robbed a collection somewhere—I don't care. They put it on the market. But they're playing it close. They print photos of a few of the best pieces, send this out to selected dealers, and no name on the folder. See that? They tell the dealers that potential buyers have to come to Egypt to see the rest of the collection and make an offer. Secretive. They think they won't get caught."

"We can put the Cairo police on it..."

"Sam, you were born yesterday. You have to play like a buyer till you get to the master mind. Who knows? It may be a new ring that's just getting started. A syndicate. How the hell do we know? With all the electronic equipment they have they can find anything these days. Just discovered ninety pieces of jewelry in a tomb *wall*. Did you read about that? *Inside the wall*."

"We can send someone on it."

"And you know who that someone is."

They both stop. The room becomes silent.

Sam closes his eyes. "Oh, no! No you don't! Barry is about to leave for Australia on the Great Barrier Reef project."

"He's leaving for Cairo."

"Kelly, we just can't—I mean, we... The Australian thing is heating up..."

"Where is he?"

"Kelly, please—."

"Where is he?"

"The wedding. Wyoming. Joe and Julie Muck."

"When's it over?"

"I'll find out."

Kelly plants her feet squarely in front of his desk. "You get Barry to Cairo as fast as you can. Call Maybelle Cartwright. Old friend of mine. She's got connections with archeologists. Don't tell her what you're up to. Just tell her Barry's coming."

"Then what?"

"I'm going back to Juergen's tomorrow. I told him I had a young couple I wanted to look over this new stuff and buy it for me. That'll be Joe and Julie."

"They have a honeymoon coming up. Surely, you can't just—."

"Send them to Abu Simbel. That's where I went on *my* honeymoon. Get them to Cairo to wait for instructions. And keep it secret. Don't tell anyone but Barry. I want him and them to dig so far into this thing they'll nab the whole goddamned outfit. Send a message that the civilized world is sick and tired of this and will no longer tolerate—."

"The civilized world loves to loot, Kelly. It's a competition."

She slaps his desk and whirls around. "Then it's by God time to *stop* it!"

She marches out and slams the door. Sam leaps to save the alabaster figurine from falling off his desk.

NINE

Julie sat back and said: "So that's what's behind this!"

Joe frowned. "Kelly went back to Bigelow?"

"The next day. She expressed interest, said she had a couple named Muck, relatives of hers—she lied there, but she wanted to show she was serious—and what should she do next? He told her he'd be in touch."

"Any idea whom he contacted?"

"Dealers are cagey. They become close-mouthed when there's a hint of illegal merchandise. They don't divulge their contacts. They could be, shall we say, eliminated."

Joe said quickly: "So could we."

Julie: "Well, if they deal in the sale of illegal stuff, aren't they subject to arrest?"

"That's why you're here in Egypt. Bigelow's not selling anything. He's just referring. He has no absolute knowledge that the stuff is illegal. If it sells, he'll get a percentage."

Joe shook his head. "I don't relate. When does he get his cut?"

"Joe, there are more secret tunnels in this business than in a prairie dog town."

He grinned again. "Did I ever tell you about that huge prairie dog town on the Sweetwater? I went down there once—."

I interrupted. "I want to hear about it. Save it. Omar's outside by now, though. I have to go."

Joe asked: "How do you plan to proceed?"

I stopped. Joe knew he couldn't get away with a question like that. "How would you proceed?"

Joe dipped into his own plan. "We wait. But not forever. If we don't hear in a year, we go home."

Julie nudged his shoulder. "A year?"

"Yeah," he answered. "I like Egypt."

"We haven't seen anything of it yet."

"Club Med and the Nile. Is there something else?"

She cuffed him again. "We're going to the Egyptian Museum and the Papyrus Museum this afternoon."

"Actually," I said, "I want you to see more of it. Fly to Aswan tomorrow. Take one of the round trip tourist flights from there to Abu Simbel."

"What's there?"

"Four colossal statues, each about twenty meters high, of Rameses II. He was a real god in his own lifetime. The place is far up the Nile. Southern boundary of Egypt in ancient times."

Julie interrupted. "I've seen pictures of them. What was the whole idea?"

"A warning. Maybe it's like our own case. If anybody came down the river and saw those statues, he'd be frightened away. Someone may be trying to frighten us away."

"How?"

"Cobras in bed is one way. That was aimed straight at me."

I reminded them that in modern times, when the Aswan dam was built, Abu Simbel was destined to be drowned in the waters of Lake Nasser. UNESCO mounted a huge campaign in 1963 to get the whole complex moved. "Got forty million dollars before they were done. The statues and a smaller temple nearby were sawed into sections, lifted to high ground, and put back together. Quite a good job, really."

Joe responded: "Then what you're saying is that we can expect to be cut to pieces here in Egypt, and then put back together."

I couldn't suppress a laugh. "Joe, you're smart. And if we are to get out of Egypt, you're going to have to stay smart. Every step of the way."

Joe: "Where are you going now? What's your long range plan?"

I told them I wasn't sure. "Once I've examined Turki's apartment, I may have some leads."

Joe: "And when we get back to Aswan?"

"Hire a felucca—."

"What's that?"

"Tall sailboat. Hire a crew, and tell them you want to sail down to Kom Ombo for overnight. Got that? Write it down. I'll join you."

Julie: "What about Philae? Edfu? Thebes?"

Barry grinned. "Stop reading the guidebooks. When we're finished you can come back and have your honeymoon. Meanwhile, we have work to do. Tell the desk here at Club Med where you are going, and that you'll be back in three days. If someone calls to set up an appointment, they'll get suspicious if you can't be found. People on the other side of the law get edgy easily."

Joe: "What if they call tonight?"

"Tell them you're booked to Aswan and will be back in three days."

"That's stalling. That tells them we are waiting to bring the cops in on the deal. Our heads could be on a brass platter for that."

"Julie's won't. Just yours."

"Thanks."

"They'll wait. They're anxious to sell you this stuff. They want your money."

Julie raised a sticky point. "What if we don't want the tomb stuff?"

"Then both your heads will be on the platter. You'd better want it. Did Kelly give you a blank check?"

"Yes."

"Well, the robbers won't have much choice. In you they have a customer. They'll wait. Be firm."

Joe said: "You sound like you know what's going to happen."

I told him I didn't. "I know human nature."

Joe asked: "What if they get mad?"

"They can get vicious, brutal, and bloody very fast. In the underworld over here there are no laws whatever. No second chances. You can get wiped out, cut to ribbons, and fed to crocodiles. That removes all evidence. I'm warning you now that this can all come unexpectedly, when you least expect it. You may find yourselves in one hell of a pickle at any time. Heads on the block, I think they call it."

Joe covered his eyes. "I want to go back to the Sweetwater."

"Let me also warn you both, that you will have to get out of whatever you get into. How good an actor are you?"

"Everybody's an actor at times," Julie said.

With this I went to the door.

"Exactly. I have interrogations in upper Egypt. See you in Aswan."

TEN

Looking outside from the window of Turki Husseini's apartment, I could just see the tops of the Pyramids. Inside there was utter chaos.

I couldn't tell much about his way of life, private or public, by the apartment he had, or the possessions in it. Books, cups, papers, pencils, clothes and other debris lay scattered all over the apartment.

"This his normal way of filing things?" I asked Omar, tongue in cheek.

Samaan shook his head and frowned. "This work of professionals."

"Looking for something, evidently. Did Turki have an office?"

"Yes. But I tell you, Barry. No one keeps anything at office. Nothing valuable, at least. Important things would be here."

"Well, they may be gone now. We're too late."

Samaan asked: "What you looking for?"

I could only answer in a cryptic vein. "Won't know till I find it."

We went to work. Omar picked up scattered clippings from Cairo newspapers. "Archeology research," he said.

We found maps, mostly hydrologic maps of the desert regions of Egypt. "Is there water out in the desert?" I inquired.

"Very little," he answered. "Oases. Spring or two. Some wadis have water running in them when rain come."

"Underground water?"

"Yes. Some places you dig in sand and get drink. Not much. You must know where to look."

"Any tombs in the desert?"

"Who knows?"

"What do you mean by that?"

"Well, Barry, we have five thousand years of blowing sand. Could be anything buried out there. The Sphinx was up to its chin in sand until little while ago."

"I get your point."

I came across maps of historic desert trails and caravan routes. What did this have to do with Turki's work? Most appeared to be photocopied from books or very old documents. The pile yielded a book on the Ice Age, tea bags, a broken tea cup, a teapot, an instrument for measuring distances on maps, full and empty Coke bottles, a sun hat, a torn and rumpled military knapsack made of heavy khaki cloth...

The Ice Age? How far back did his curiosity go? The Swains had said that Egyptian history went back 700,000 years. The glacier came only ten thousand years ago. I was getting more confused by the minute.

Picking up the Ice Age book, I thumbed through it. Glacial geology, moraines, giant ripples, maximum extent of the ice, migration of plants and animals. Basic stuff. Why would anyone in Egypt want a book on the Ice Age ten thousand years ago? I asked Omar about it. He answered, almost absent-mindedly. "You need go to university."

He was right. That's where the experts were. I picked up a piece of scrap paper with one word written on it. "What's this?"

Omar came over and glanced at the paper. "Upuat?"

I asked him if it was Arabic.

"No. I never see this word before."

After making some notes, I saw that I would have to come back, so I asked Omar if he intended to seal this room.

"Yes."

"Then I'll leave everything here."

Where a desk had been knocked over I found paper clips, pens, pencils, calling cards, keys, small and large envelopes, and a compass.

"Omar, do you know if Turki drove a car?"

"I think so. Government car."

"Did he have a personal car?"

"I don't think so. He didn't need one. Want me to check?"

"No. But here's something else. A piece of note paper with a name and time on it. 'Amir, 2 p.m. Friday.' Make anything of that?"

"Maybe. Maybe. Let me see. Amir. We have a pilot by that name. He fly helicopters."

"Government pilot?"

"Military, I think."

"And he could have flown Turki around, from dig to dig?"

Omar shook his head. "I don't know. Could be."

"Out into the desert?"

"Anywhere. What you talking about?"

"Well, judging by all the maps, he had an unusual interest in the desert. Any idea what he might have been after?"

"I'm a policeman."

"I mean, no stories about him in the newspapers? Feature articles on him or his work?"

"Barry, government peoples very secret. Turki tomb man. We have many tombs. He wouldn't want anyone out there, maybe digging without he knows."

"Good point, Omar."

A pile of booklets caught my eye. *Explorations Géologiques et Hydrologiques des Wadis Égyptiennes.* Why would Turki be so interested in the wadis and other dry stream beds of the desert?

Another book: *Gouvernements Dynastiques de l'Égypte Ancienne.* Turki was after something about the makeup and operation of ancient dynasties. Another book described *Investigative Methods and Field Techniques*, published by an American university.

I was impressed. The guy could read French and English as well as Arabic, and I remarked on this to Omar.

He smiled. "Teachers tell us if we get to be important, we have to learn many languages. Mainly English."

"Turki also wrote all his notes, it appears, in English. Why not Arabic?"

"Oh, simple, very simple. We do that to keep secrets from other people. If Turki had important secrets, and something happen to him, he want secrets to be discovered by English-speaking people."

"Logical," I commented, "and yet strange. And not terribly practical. I'll have to meditate on that..."

Another booklet: *Renseignements Pratiques sur les Investigations Archéologiques de l'Égypte.* I spoke softly. "Practical Information on Archeological Investigations in Egypt. Pretty clear, I'd say. This guy was searching for something ..."

Omar said: "Maybe he found it."

This thought had been occurring to me with maddening frequency. "Well, if so, it was a hell of a big find. What he found was so valuable that he was murdered for it."

Omar looked at me. "Not unusual in history of crime, huh?"

I thought for a moment. "Tell me something else, Omar. You're Egyptian. Turki had an annoying penchant for getting people mad at him. Is that customary in the government?"

"How can I answer? He was a human being."

"Okay. That says a lot. Still, he wasn't very diplomatic.

Or else he was too occupied with desert wadis and the Ice Age. He neglected the people whose work he was supposed to be supervising. That party at Maybelle's. We have a couple dozen suspects, people so mad at him they might have knifed him. They should have been friends for whom he would do anything. Something doesn't add up here."

"Never does at first," Omar observed. "Why not?"

"Well, the curious thing is that none of the things here—the Ice Age material, hydrologic maps and so on— relates to the work of any of Maybelle's archeologists. Not as far as I can tell, anyway."

"Yes...?"

"He was after something on his own."

Samaan laughed. "Egyptians will try everything on the side to make some extra money."

"So will Americans," I answered. "You know anyone who wouldn't?"

I probed further, trying to find some order in all this debris. A torn wrapper from a package with the return address "Deutsches Generalkonsulat, Alexandria-Rouschdy." Rumpled correspondence to "Ägyptisches Fremdenverkehrsamt" in Frankfurt, Germany.

I mentioned this to Omar. "He had connections with the Germans."

"Germans very interested in Egypt."

Statuettes, family photos, a booklet on specialized computer programs. Reports on Sanford Santano's work, but nothing else from Maybelle's group. She'd said Sandy was a favorite of Turki's.

"Omar," I said, with a feeling of disappointment, "There are some things that ought to be here and are not..."

"What, for example?"

"Files, folders, letters. He must have had a lot of correspondence, man in his position."

"You can look in files of his bureau."

"Perhaps. You said that valuable things would be kept at home. His files could have been stolen."

"Depends on what thieves wanted, no?"

"Guns? Knives?"

"He wouldn't need them. He was archeologist, not policeman."

"Food?"

"Ate in a restaurant. No time to cook meals."

"Money? A wallet?"

"First things to be stolen..."

My shoulders drooped. "Omar, you haven't given me any answers at all."

Omar grinned. "Ah, but Barry, it is I who am looking to *you* for answers."

ELEVEN

As soon as the plane landed in Aswan that afternoon, I placed a call on the military satellite digital network to Washington. The response was instant and clear.

"Good morning. Barry Ross's office. Della Smith. May I help you?"

What a cheerful voice. I never ceased to be refreshed by it.

"Good afternoon, Della—."

"Oh, Barry! I'm glad you called. They've been steadily trying to get hold of you from Cairns. The area of dying corals is spreading from Dinkum Island to other parts of the Great Barrier Reef. And they have no leads on the two murdered biologists. They want you there right away."

I knew it would happen. Every time I call Della I run into trouble. "All right, first tell them to call Dr. Brasher and—."

"He's the one trying to get in touch with you."

"Then call him back and tell him I'm up to my ears in tombs and I've got a murder here to solve. There's no way I can leave for Australia until—well, hell, I don't know when I'll break out of here. Then keep him posted."

She jotted some notes, then said: "Hounto Chala called from Nairobi. He wants you to take one of the UNEP officials through the Grand Canyon."

I winced. "You're kidding?"

"It's set for next June 20."

"What does my calendar look like?"

"Bad. Mño called last night from Caracas..."

"Never mind about Mño."

"Shall I tell him that?"

"No. Tell him I couldn't be reached in Egypt, but I'll try to get to Caracas as soon as I can after Australia. Ask the State Department or Interior to take over Chala's guy. I'd like to do it, but I can't get into operating a guide service."

"He says you did such a good job of taking him through the canyon that he wants you to take this other guy."

"Chala was the head honcho. If I take everyone on his staff down the canyon I won't have time for anything else. Keep me out of it. Tell him my schedule is impossible. No, that won't work. Give him the Chinese answer. I'll do it if I possibly can and I feel honored to be asked. Then call Interior and quietly get a substitute they can plug in at the last minute."

"Barry, you are diabolical."

"I know it."

"I'll try."

"Della, I'm in a bind and need help, fast. Check our databases, then call the State Department, CIA, Egyptian Embassy, FBI and Scotland Yard. Run down what you can on illegal syndicates that deal with Egyptian antiquities. Get names if you can. Recent history. Anything."

"I'll need a month."

"Tomorrow morning. I'm going to be in upper Egypt interrogating some people."

"Yes sir."

"How are you, Della?"

"Fine, Barry. How are you?"

"Frustrated. But I like Egypt."

"Good. I'll get to work."

I powered off.

TWELVE

As soon as Julie and Joe returned to Aswan from Abu Simbel, we went down to the docks on the Nile.

Walking up the planks and down the steps into the felucca, Julie and Joe were all eyes, scanning the sail that rose high overhead, the intricate pattern of ropes, the narrow carpeted deck some thirty feet long. Then they settled on a soft bench at the railing, turned and looked across the Nile past other tall, white sails to the high bank where stood the Mausoleum of the Aga Khan.

They were full of questions. What had happened? Where do we stand? Did they always use feluccas on the Nile?

I ignored their questions. Why should I answer? The Nile didn't care. Why should I?

Julie harrumphed. "Barry. You're mean."

"All right, if you have to know. Rafts. Primitive rafts. Made from the stalks of papyrus plants. There wasn't much wood around here for boat building. Maybe they imported big logs from upstream. I've seen paintings in the tombs that show fishermen in boats and rafts. Then there are paintings of big ceremonial boats that carried the pharaohs and other high government officials."

▼▼▼▼▼▼▼▼▼▼▼▼▼▼▼▼▼▼▼▼▼▼▼▼▼▼▼▼▼▼▼▼▼▼▼▼▼▼▼

I paused. My mind went back to the days of the elegant courts, trying to perceive what Turki Husseini was after. There was no connection, no clue, nothing.

Oh, yes there is, my inner voice told me. *Everything is connected to everything, remember. You said so yourself.*

"The earliest known boat here is one found in a causeway near the Pyramids, which would date it at about 2,400 B.C. As soon as they had any international commerce, especially with Palestine and Greece, the Egyptians had to design more sturdy ships like the dhow, a sailboat designed for the open sea. Here on the Nile, the felucca became the principal sailing vessel. Winds are usually less violent and waves more gentle. There, my lecture for the day is over. Class dismissed."

Joe, as usual, hung on to every word. "If a wind comes up tonight," he said, looking up at the ungainly sail, "we swim to Kom Ombo."

I tried to reassure them that the craft was pretty steady, for all its looks. We couldn't deny how graceful all the others looked as they made their way across the river.

The boatmen took up the planks and hauled in the ropes, then cast off, steering the felucca gently out into the Nile. The three of us leaned back against carpets piled along the sides of the boat. Joe lay with hands under the back of his head as he pondered the huge sail towering above, lighted softly by the afternoon sun.

"You know," he said lazily, "I could get used to this."

Julie looked at me. "He's getting spoiled. I won't be able to do a thing with him when we get back to our home in Wyoming."

"What home in Wyoming?" Joe asked, glazed eyes fixed on the sails. "I've forgotten all about it."

"Well," I said, "this will wake you up. Want to know what I found in Turki's apartment?"

"Sure," Julie replied. "I asked you at the airport."

"Well, the answer is nothing."

"That's something," she said.

"No, it isn't. If he kept something there, someone got it. The place looked like Joe's room at the ranch."

"That bad?" she asked.

"Really bad. But I did find some stuff. Lots of books on the Ice Age and hydrology."

"Wait," Julie said. "You don't need to study hydrology along the Nile. That must be very well known already. He apparently was searching for something out in the desert."

I was astounded at her sudden grasp of the situation. "Smart, Julie. Tell me more."

"Well, if he's trying to study modern hydrology, I don't see the point. The deserts we've flown over are dry as a bone."

"So, what's the point then?"

"If he wasn't trying to decipher modern hydrology, then he was trying to decipher ancient hydrology."

"All right," I responded. "That brings you up to where I've gotten lost. Why was he trying to decipher ancient hydrology?"

She lay back on the carpet and looked up into the sail. "That's the end of my lecture for today. Class dismissed."

I asked them about Abu Simbel.

"Just as you described it," Julie responded. "Amazing."

"What I can't understand," Joe commented, coming back awake, "is how in the name of thunder a fantastic civilization could spring up out of the desert and be so arty, so skilled, and build all those monuments, haul all these rocks, cut all that granite."

My mind was doing double duty. I tried to think of the past as it related to Joe's questions, and the past as it related to Turki Husseini. The answer to my own questions was in there somewhere and I had to try to get to it. "One simple reason," I answered. "They had time."

"Huh?"

"Time. Every year when the Nile flooded they sat back and watched as new layers of silt settled over their fields and fertilized the soil for them. Then they planted and crops thrived…vegetables, beans, grapes, grains, dates…They harvested. They had plenty of water, few storms, no tornadoes, hurricanes. They had fish, wild fowl…as close to paradise as you can imagine."

"The people originally came downstream?"

I had to pass on that question. "The first real civilizations sprang up in Mesopotamia, just to the northeast of today's Iraq. Lots of water there, then, and forests. After the Ice Age, the Sahara Desert probably had lots of water and—."

I stopped in mid-sentence.

What had I said?

My eyes focused on the treeless desert beyond the river's edge. Rocky. Empty. Stretching as far as we could see.

Joe asked: "What's the matter? What do you see?"

I scarcely heard him. I went silent, my mind whirling.

"What's the matter with you?" he asked.

When I finally spoke, it seemed as though my voice came from up somewhere above the sail.

"The springs and oases had not entirely dried up by 5,000 years ago."

Julie became curious. She sat up. "What did you say? What is that supposed to mean?"

I went on, talking aloud to myself rather than to them. "As the water began to disappear, people must have begun moving from the deserts toward the rivers. Toward the Nile, a permanent source of water. They began to develop into societies and became cultured by the time of the first dynasties. Tab and Veronica Swain are studying pre-pharaonic Egypt and they think those people were fascinating. But I don't see what that has to do with Turki's efforts."

"Well," Julie said. "Turn that whole situation around. You're only talking about people moving from the desert to the Nile."

"What are you trying to say?"

She held up her hand, as though to say: "Wait, I'm trying to think."

The mast creaked as the felucca floated slowly down the river. On shore, a small green line of vegetation separated the river from the utterly grassless expanse beyond. An empty barge trudged with a gentle putt-putt up the river toward Aswan.

I fell into deep thought, reflecting on the two and two I had just put together. There may not have been any connection, but I couldn't help drifting back to what Egypt might have been like in the time of Amenemhet.

Julie and Joe lay with eyes closed, lulled by the creaking timbers, half asleep. I let them rest. They had had little relaxation since the wedding. For perhaps half an hour they napped, caught up in the mesmerizing drift of the vessel.

Julie waked and sat up. "What if people were going from the Nile out into the desert?"

Joe responded. "Go back to sleep. Why would anyone in his right mind want to leave the gardens of the Nile and go out to live in the desert? There's no food out there. No water. No wet bars. Come on. That's murder."

She lay back down without answering.

Joe's mind never seemed to stop. "Well, if they came out of the desert, formed empires—."

"Dynasties," Julie corrected.

"So what about these dynasties? I'm confused. Abu Simbel was not the work of a primitive tribe. Who was Rameses?"

"The ancient Egyptians," I said, trying to set him straight, "had more than four hundred kings during their history, which ended about 495 A.D. One of the earliest pharaohs was Djoser. He built the step pyramid at Saqqara, the oldest known building of its size in the world. Then in the fourth dynasty, the great pyramids near Giza were built. Largest edifices ever built by human hands, some say, but I would confer that honor on the Great Wall of China. No matter, the Pyramids were fantastic accomplishments for nearly five thousand years ago."

"Where did Tut fit in?"

"A minor king. He died young."

"Rameses?"

"There were eleven in that line. The one you're talking about was Rameses the second. He had more buildings and colossal statues built than anyone else. He was a god in his own time."

Julie sat enrapt. "Get to Cleopatra," she urged.

"No, wait," Joe said. "I'm trying to find out if there's any connection between any of these dynasties and the desert out there. They could have been attacked from hordes coming out of those deserts."

"They were," I said. "Egypt was always rife with conspiracies. I can't name a culture that wasn't. Like modern times."

"So?"

"The country was invaded, plundered, and captured by outsiders, then freed again. Eventually Alexander the Great took over and Egypt was ruled by the Greeks. Then the Romans. After that the Christians came in and tried to deface every temple they could find."

"No, no… This is not what I'm getting at. If these pharaohs were so powerful and so smart…they could do anything."

"Not quite. Brace yourself, Joe. The Egyptians never invented the wheel. They never had coins. They didn't even have camels. Got all these from outsiders. They got fouled up in intrigues. Cleopatra lived in the tumultuous time of the Romans and finally had to kill herself."

Joe shook his head. "You're missing my point. We're not getting anywhere. But somewhere in here is the secret we're looking for."

The creaking of the masts, the gentle ripple of water, almost mesmerized me. The raucous cities faded away. The shouts of merchants were silenced and out of memory. Now the world was only the water, a fringe of green, and the desert. Not even a call of the muezzin from his tower.

My eyes sagged for a moment. Then I looked downstream.

"There it is."

"What, the secret?"

"No. Kom Ombo."

Julie turned in her seat. Joe rolled over on his side.

The building, set against the softened sun, rose like a low and massively constructed castle on the bank of the Nile. Like a bold intrusion, outpost of a monumental past, here on the quiet bank of the modern river. Kom Ombo was a favorite with me, so lonely out here in the farmlands and desert. As though someone in a distant celestial sphere had caressed the earth and left behind this loving and heartfelt tribute to the gods of yore. The crocodile and the hawk. The love and fear of animals in ancient times. The respect. That swayed me more than anything.

"Joe," I said, "that place is a pantheon of the gods. If you have any connections, now's the time."

He slumped. "I give up."

THIRTEEN

The fading sun turned the temple red as we entered its lofty, ruined halls, strolled among giant pillars, and stopped beneath grand bas-reliefs. I pointed out Hathor, the hawk-headed god, and Sobek, the crocodile-headed god.

"They would have your answers," I said.

We were interrupted by a young Chinese woman in field clothing.

"Mei Hua!" I said, taking her hands. "What a nice surprise. Here, I want you to meet some tourists, Mr. and Mrs. Muck. This is Mei Hua, who is researching the colors in these ancient monuments."

Joe seemed astonished. "They had color?"

"Yes," said Mei Hua, in her sweet soft voice. "Very much of it. Look up there."

On the north side of a tall column they saw remnants of red and blue in the grooves of hieroglyphs.

"Mineral colors," Mei Hua said. "Five thousand years ago. All other colors faded in desert sun."

As Julie and Joe wandered out into a courtyard of columns, I took Mei Hua aside. "I am trying to find out more about Turki. Did he ever mention to you anything about research he was doing on his own?"

"No," she answered. "He always gave us idea that he had to spend full time following us around."

"Did he follow you around?"

"No."

"He never came to where you worked?"

"No."

'He listened to your reports at Maybelle's?"

"Yes."

"Read your field notes?"

"I don't know. He never talked about them. Maybelle did."

"Did he ever talk about the desert, out toward Libya?"

She seemed a little surprised by the question. "No."

"Did he ever, at Maybelle's, brief you on other research under way in Egypt."

"No."

"Anything to do with hydrologic systems, underground water, ancient springs, wadis...?"

"No."

"Thank you, Mei Hua. This has been helpful."

"But I have told you nothing."

"You've told me more than you think."

"Do you know who killed Mr. Husseini?"

"Yes, I think I do. But I don't know how. Or where. I have much to do yet."

She bowed politely and said: "Gei nin xing fu."

"Thank you, Mei Hua. Xie xie. I'll need all the luck I can get."

"I help you any time," she said, and disappeared into the shadows.

FOURTEEN

We slept that night on the carpets in the felucca. Joe watched the light of stars, filtered through the haze, and vowed to lie back and watch for hours, "meditating on the universe," as he said. He lasted only five minutes.

My mind went back to Mei Hua and what she had told me. Turki Husseini did not take these people into his confidence. I couldn't get around it. That was fact number one. That's where I had to start. There was something he did not want them to know, did not want *anyone* to know.

If he worked on something else, something secret and important, that might explain why he all but neglected Maybelle's archeologists. Why he angered them so much. He must have been simply drifting away...

Next morning, a speed boat picked us up by prearrangement and before long we arrived at Luxor. I wanted Julie and Joe to see Karnak, so we took a horse-drawn carriage to this most important temple complex in Egypt. Entering past rows of ram-headed sphinxes, we wandered among walls, pylons, obelisks, columns, and statues. Then among the gigantic decorated columns of hypostyle halls, which seemed to diminish the stature of modern visitors to the size of a mouse.

After that we toured the massive temple of Luxor, with its multiple columns and colossal statues of Rameses II. And another hawk, deified in granite.

Reboarding our carriage, we returned to the Nile, and caught a ferry to the west side of the river. Climbing up the bank, I pointed out a long low structure ahead.

"That's Medinet Habu. Rameses III built a mortuary temple there. The place was also an administrative center because this area was once the capital of all Egypt. Talk about color: you walk through the doorways and look up, and you see complex designs with the original colors intact. Mei Hua works on her colors there."

Joe frowned. "Now what does all that have to do with us?"

I turned my head and looked away. "Joe, there's a connection in here somewhere. There's a link. Turki found it. We have to find it."

"You said this was the capital of Egypt for a while?"

"Yes."

"Well, if it's like Washington, the greatest intrigues would be here. This is where the pharaohs lived. This where all the guys climbing for power would gather and try to depose them. Am I getting through to you?"

"Joe, you have one thing right. Their governments must have had a lot of similarities to ours. Now tell us how that relates to Turki Husseini."

Joe slumped. "I wanna go back to Wyoming."

We hired a car and drove south, toward a grand colonnaded structure at the base of a high cliff. "That's my favorite," I said. "Deir-el-Bahri. One of the world's greatest masterpieces of architecture. Long ramps. Terraces. Causeways. Temples. All built in harmony with the rock cliffs behind."

Joe said: "Looks like something out of *Lost Horizon*."

I added: "Hatshepsut had a big hand in building it when she was queen."

Julie: "Of course. That's why it has such an elegant touch."

Following the signs to Biban el-Muluk, we entered
the Valley of the Kings, an arid, grassless canyon set far
back and hidden from the Nile.

"Sixty-two tombs here," I said, "far as anyone knows.
From Tuthmosis I to Rameses XI, including Tutankhamun,
the last to be discovered. But what really grabs you is the
intricate paintings on the walls as you go down the steps
deep into the ground. They hold a lot of secrets. Sandy
Santano's here. I'm going to see him. Why don't you visit
Tut's tomb while I'm doing that?"

FIFTEEN

We split up. Joe and Julie joined a line to descend into Tut's tomb. I went up the hill to the tomb of Seti I, showed my badge to a guard, and walked down the long corridor in almost total blackness. Dim lights soon showed, and I came to Sandy's group working with cameras, computers, and digital machines.

"Sandy, I will interrupt your work for only a moment or two."

"Barry, I am at your command. I want to see Turki's murderer apprehended."

"You liked him, did you not?"

"He helped me get all this equipment and gave me free rein down here. I like all Egyptians."

"I admire that, Sandy. And Turki liked you and your work?"

"I think so."

"Did he ever discuss any other projects with you?"

"You mean projects the Swains were working on? Mei Hua? Hami? No."

"How about *beyond* Maybelle's group? Did he ever talk about anything he himself had under way? Any research project going on elsewhere in Egypt?"

Sandy thought for a moment, eyes on the dim figures of Egyptian history painted on the softly lighted wall. "As a matter of fact, he did. He made what I thought were some rather strange inquiries."

"Yes?"

"He asked if I had ever detected any references to…to members of the pharaohs' staffs, king's orderlies, stuff like that."

"You answered in the affirmative?"

"Yes. These paintings tell a lot about everyday life, and about people other than the pharaohs. Fishermen. Farmers. Hunters. Scribes…You've seen them."

"Any particular period?"

"Amenemhet mostly, I think."

"Did you wonder why he should be interested in people working for the pharaohs?"

"It seemed a little odd. I asked him about it. He never really opened up much to anyone, so I dropped it. I felt that he thought my researches had some answers to his inquiries. But he was still secretive. If I asked him what he was doing, he deflected my question and asked another one."

I listened intently, then: "What did he ask you?"

"Had I seen any references to oases and arid lands? I didn't know what he was getting at. There are lots of both in Egypt. I couldn't figure out what he meant, and I said so. He asked about any possible maps in the drawings, trade routes to Libya—."

I interrupted. "Did he say Libya? You're certain?"

"Yeah. But I couldn't help him. And that was the last time I talked with him."

"When was that?"

"A week ago, maybe."

I shook hands with him. "Sandy, you've been a world of help."

"I have?"

"Turki opened up to you. It must have been about the closest he confided to anyone about his big secret."

"What are you talking about?"

"He was working on something involving the wadis to the west. Something during the years after the glacial period ended. Hydrology. There would have been more water out there in the desert five thousand years ago."

"What do you think he was after? Ancient trade routes, roads?"

"I haven't the slightest idea yet, but I'm getting closer. I'll keep you posted."

"Thanks, Barry."

SIXTEEN

Climbing back up to the surface, I entered the tomb of Rameses VI and found Hasmukhlal Gandhi, angry as ever. He showed me some of the original masterpieces falling off the walls and onto the floor. "Have you time to see more of this, farther back?"

"Sorry," I replied, "wish I had. Can you restore those things?"

"Oh, some have been pasted back. Others have been lost forever. I call it quite disgraceful. No one wants to study cracks in the walls."

"Except you. Are you progressing?"

"I'm finding causes. But there's so much. Luxor Temple was in very poor condition before they restored it."

"I've just come from Sandy's operation in Seti I's tomb. I marvel at what he's capturing on film and disc."

"That's good. But ground water is rising up into the temples..."

"Ground water?"

"I'm working on hydrologic cycles here in the Valley of the Kings. If we could channel some of this moisture elsewhere—."

I moved closer and asked, in a confidential tone, "Hami, tell me quite frankly. Did Turki Husseini ever discuss hydrologic cycles with you?"

Hami registered surprise. "Why, yes, he did. Very secretly, I should say. As though he were holding back something. How did you know?"

"He was very interested in hydrologic patterns in certain areas. Did he discuss ground water with you, its effect
on tombs, things like that?"

"Barry, I can't actually say that we discussed anything.
Turki wasn't like that. He didn't seem to care what I was
doing...Or what I thought."

"Isn't that odd? I mean, you're trying to restore crum-
bling tombs."

"Yes, but he asked about ground water in what seemed
to me a rather disinterested manner."

"Sounds like a subterfuge. Hami, he wasn't disinterested at all. He was really trying to mask something else.
He didn't want anyone on his trail."

Hami frowned. "Barry, are you serious? If so, you must
be on to something. I don't quite understand."

"Well, he apparently had some kind of secret project
going on. It involved hydrology of certain basins, wadis,
oases, I don't know. Possibly, in the direction of Libya. Did
he ever mention any of that to you?"

Hami thought for a moment. "He never inferred he
was doing something on his own. He projected the picture
of a public servant dedicated to protecting Egyptian antiquities. All he asked me was the reference sources of my studies on ground water. At the time, I thought it rather an idle
question."

"Perhaps it was, but I don't think so. Anything else?
Any other departures from normal supervision or your ac-
tivities?"

"Come to think of it, he once asked if I'd seen any
paintings or hieroglyphic writings on—how shall I phrase
it?—the lesser staffs beneath the pharaohs."

"Did he really?"

"He seemed to be after what we would call bureau
chiefs, viziers, the like."

"What did you tell him?"

"I felt a little silly. He surely knew as much as I. It's common knowledge how scribes and other officials are frequently pictured in these paintings. I ran through the whole lot again, what I'd seen, where I saw it. He asked which specific dynasties. That, too, is well known. The lives of the Egyptians for centuries are plainly illustrated in color paintings on all these walls...or, I should say, what's left of these walls."

"He was interested in the desert. Did he ever ask about oases?"

Hami thought for a moment and frowned again. "I have to confess that when I see paintings of geese flying, I just assume it's along the Nile. Perhaps some could as well have been in oases. He may have asked about oases. I simply can't remember at the moment."

"What about wadis? Stream beds? Water distribution out on the desert? You're into that here, are you not?"

"Yes, I am. And yes, he took an interest in subsurface water as it relates to surface features."

This brought me to attention. "You're sure?"

"Quite so. I deal with that ever so much, you know. I merely thought he was interested from my point of view, not his."

"Did what you answered seem to satisfy him?"

Hami shook his head and grinned. "One never knew that about Turki. He lived in his own world."

"I'm beginning to see that. Anything else?"

"Not that I can recall."

"Thank you, Hami."

"For what? Have I helped?"

"I don't know yet, but I think so. Oh, one other question. Have you heard of any discoveries of artifacts in tombs lately, private or otherwise?"

"A curious question, Barry. You'll never hear of private discoveries, even after they're sold. Too dangerous. Illegal. There was the discovery of items in the wall of a tomb recently. But the government was in on that. Otherwise ..."

'Have you ever heard of syndicates robbing, stealing, selling?"

"Afraid not, Barry." He gave a short laugh. "My experience with the underground is rather limited to the Valley of the Kings."

I was about to leave when I remembered something else. "By the way, I came across a piece of paper in his apartment that had the word 'Upuat' on it. That mean anything to you?"

"Yes, Barry. I've heard of it. That is a little television camera which the Germans brought down to use in the pyramids. The camera is mounted on a kind of tiny cart, with outsized wheels that have good traction."

"What did they use it for?"

"There were some long shafts that angled upward in the pyramids, too small for human beings to enter. They sent the little camera, which had a light on the front, up those shafts to photograph any possible objects. Long cables fed the signal back down to a monitor at the bottom of the shaft so the researchers could follow the progress of the little explorer."

"Did they find anything?"

"I don't recall. Probably some technical revelations. The shafts may have been merely for ventilation."

"Did Turki ever mention this device to you?"

"Not that I remember. I talked to the Germans about it."

"Turki had no plans to get one for your use...or his?"

"He never mentioned it to me."

"How do you think he would have used one?"

"Barry, the first thought that comes to my mind, is to run the little camera into holes in walls or caves. That way, you could see if there are tombs inside that the ancient Egyptians might have tried to seal shut. You wouldn't actually have to enlarge the opening, or roll big rocks away, to find out what was inside."

This stopped me cold. My mind exploded in twenty different directions, but I tried not to let on. I thanked Hami, urged him to keep up the good work, and left.

SEVENTEEN

I was now more confused than ever. Turki Husseini had been pursuing a theme...if not a dream. He brought up the same queries to different people in different ways and tapped them for insights into his own projects.

What was he doing? He evidently never told anyone. Not even Sandy Santano, with whom he seemed to have the closest friendship. I could understand his being close-mouthed. He must have had lots of secrets.

What bothered me most was that the guy never seemed to have written any of this down. Or if he did, it had been stolen. I tried again and again to unleash my mind and to put myself in his place. If I had discovered something really overwhelming, I wouldn't broadcast it to the entire world, either.

Until...Well, until when? And why wait?

It would take years to get anything published in a journal. If I were doing it, I would write out some notes now and then, and stash them away where nobody could find them. Did he keep a daily log, perhaps? A field notebook? Letters to somebody? Memos to a colleague?

Now I discover, through Hami, that he was interested in a little device that could go into holes and tell you what was inside. Meaning also, go into caves. Could he have come upon some suspicious caves and was trying to get into them? Caves in the desert? Toward Libya? Toward Palestine? Which dynasty? Or dynasties? Which pharaoh? Vizier? Scribe?

My alter ego was becoming impatient. *If all you have is questions, you dum-dum, you're not going to get very far. For a hot-shot investigator, you are about to become a washout unless you find someone who knows something. Anything...*

I scarcely spoke to Julie and Joe on the way back to Luxor. They saw me lost in thought, and must have wondered about it. I glanced at them. It was time to get their brains working on this.

The perpetual dust in the air, risen with the winds, lifted from the sands of the deserts on both sides of the Nile, seldom let us see blue sky. Yet it did have one advantage: glorious sunsets.

The three of us sat beside the pool at Club Med Luxor, on a terrace overlooking the Nile. In the waters a gently rippling gold shone brightly. A gold so reminiscent of the richly crafted necklaces of the kings. The cliffs to the west had turned deep purple under a bronze sky.

Deir-el-Bahri could scarcely be seen, but Julie stared at it intently. "What a woman she must have been," she said, half aloud.

"Who?" Joe asked.

"Hatshepsut. A woman leader in a man's world. A real hembra among machos. That's what I call a real woman. Look at that architecture. There must not be anything like it, anywhere..."

"I can't see it."

"I can. What grand processions they had up those ramps, beneath those columns... Costumes of gold...necklaces of turquoise..."

"You're getting carried away, Julie."

"I sure am. Don't interrupt me."

I had to break in: "I fear we must, Julie. Things are starting to come together. We have to coordinate our—."

My pocket phone vibrated. It was Della. I listened for nearly five minutes. When I put my phone back away, Joe said: "Who was that?"

"I asked Della to get me a briefing on syndicates dealing with Egyptian artifacts. She called all over, FBI, Scotland Yard, CIA."

"Any results?"

"Syndicates like we may be dealing with don't leave tracks. They don't have names. Or if they do, they change names frequently. Sales are made through code names, money laundered, and the sellers drift back into the shadows. It's like picking up a piece of water. They fall through police fingers and are gone."

"As I would have suspected," Joe said.

Julie still gazed at Deir-el-Bahri. She shook her head, as though waking from a dream. "You said things were starting to come together? What have you found?"

"Tantalizing hints. Speculation. But also a great gap."

"Gap? Between what and what?"

"I still have no idea what Turki was after. No one knows. Or no one is telling."

Joe slumped his shoulders. "Bring us up to date."

"Samaan and I went to Turki's room. It had been ransacked. Whoever did it wasn't looking for coin collections. They took away all specific details they didn't want anyone to see. I found maps and research materials galore on hydrology of the desert. Not a thing specific."

Julie asked: "Why was he so interested in ground water?"

I could only sigh helplessly. "I wish I knew."

"Springs, maybe? Oases?"

"Could be."

"But what for?"

I spread my hands. "There is a key to all this. But it wasn't in his room."

Julie asked: "What about Maybelle's group? Did you get anything out of them?"

"From Mei Hua, nothing except the fact that Turki was close-mouthed. From Hami, nothing except a few seemingly idle queries. From Sandy, a little. Sandy's working to record the paintings in the tomb of Seti I. For some reason, Turki liked him better than the others. I think it was completely impersonal, however. As near as I can detect, Sandy was actually preserving the tomb paintings and making lasting records of them. Turki liked this idea. But more than that, he was looking for something in those paintings."

"People? Places? Processes? What?"

"He asked Sandy about two things. Lesser luminaries in pharaoh administrations, and modern reference works on oases and arid lands."

Julie shook her head. "That all points to something... What do you make of it?"

"Well, since Turki rarely asked questions of anybody, for fear of letting out some sort of secret, he apparently trusted Sandy enough to make certain inquiries."

"Then he could have confided in someone else, maybe?"

"There may be someone who knows. My mind is twisted shut, but I'm open to input. Any ideas?"

Julie sat with her eyes focused on the distant shadow where Hatshepsut's temple had sunk into the purple gloom of evening. I watched her now with considerable interest. I knew she had an exceptional brain, and the ability to pierce to the heart of a subject. I wondered if now she had been stumped.

Why not? my inner voice inquired. *You brought her out of the canyons and mountains of the American West and thrust her into a place she's never seen. You lay before her a history of millenniums about which nobody has all the answers. You take her among a people she's never studied. Then you bring up questions that even you yourself can't answer. What do you expect?*

She looked around. We were alone on the terrace. The bathers had long since disappeared or gone down to happy hour and dinner. I could tell that Julie, Hatshepsut aside, had been listening and pondering. She scanned the western rim of the valley which still glowed with a delicate bronze, and spoke at last.

"Let us put ourselves in Turki's place..."

I answered: "That's where I've been for what seems like a month, and I still haven't enough to go on."

"Not that," she said. "I mean the present, or, well, the recent past."

Joe: "Explain."

Julie: "If I were Turki, and I got some fabulous idea, or made some discovery, I didn't want anyone to know about, I'd keep my mouth shut. Very, very shut..."

Joe scowled. "You're not getting anywhere..."

"Yes, I am. I've been thinking. If I were surrounded by greedy people—you said Egypt was very poor—."

I answered: "Turki wasn't poor. Not by Egyptian standards."

"No," Julie continued, "but he may have been very hungry."

Joe: "If you don't stop talking in riddles..."

She seemed not to hear him. "All right. You talk of archeologists being very anxious to discover a tomb, bring out great treasures, go down in history as a big hero. Okay?"

I said: "Call it the Howard Carter syndrome. Look what he brought to the world out of Tut's tomb."

Julie still gazed across the darkening valley. "That's what I mean. Some kind of a dream. He'd be a hero forever. He'd be in the history books, the annals of archeology..."

"So...?"

"So Turki must have fancied that he lived in a world of intrigue."

I smiled. "That's no fancy. Name of the game in this part of the world. Most parts of the world, for that matter. Julie, I've been through all this in my own mind."

"Or, worse yet," she went on, ignoring me, "a world of predatory archeologists. Like a crow that finds a piece of meat, and starts to eat it, and all the other crows swoop in to take it away."

"Like a Wall Street banker with a hot stock tip," Joe said, grinning and circling his finger in the air. "So?"

▼▼▼▼▼▼▼▼▼▼▼▼▼▼▼▼▼▼▼▼▼▼▼▼▼▼▼▼▼▼▼▼▼▼

"At the first suggestion that he was on the trail of something big, lots of people would stop at nothing to get his secret. Does anyone know if he had been tortured?"

I answered. "Samaan and I did find some burn marks. I have to confess I didn't think of torture. He could have been branded. Like a cow."

Joe, the cowboy, convulsed. "God damn, that's the awfulest thing I ever..."

We fell into silence, waiting for Julie to go on.

"Well, put yourself in Turki's mind again," she said. "If he had a terrific secret, like someone who had discovered gold, he knew that once the secret got out, there'd be a gold rush. Right? Like the crow, there would be people swooping in from all directions to take it away from him."

I was fascinated by her reasoning and kept wondering where it would lead. I said: "Keep going."

Joe interrupted: "Are you trying to say that he—?"

Julie: "I'm not saying it."

Joe: "Well, you're sure as hell *thinking* it. There's only one kind of gold rush in Egypt..."

Joe and I looked at each other. On the dimly lighted terrace, with the sun now gone, we could scarcely discern the expressions on each other's faces.

Julie said simply: "He found a tomb."

I leaned back and said: "When I went through Turki's things in his apartment, I was never very far from this possibility. The archeologists themselves admit to such a fantasy, always hoping that some day they'll go down a yellow brick road..."

"Okay," Julie continued, "if you do find one, you have three choices. One. Forget it and keep it sealed. If you do that, someone else will almost surely find it some day. Two. Take out the contents for museums. That would have brought Turki more fame than Carter got from bringing the stuff out of Tut's tomb. Three. Steal the contents and sell them."

Joe and I mulled this over silently, not quite sure what to make of it. Then Joe said: "This is a nice train of thought, but now you come to the scruples of the finder. What do we know about Turki?"

I answered that one easily. "His character, to me, is as flat as a piece of paper. Most of those who knew him seem to think he was a petty tyrant. But not necessarily a thief."

Joe: "Did they consider him a bastard for overzealous protection of Egyptian antiquities?"

"Well, sort of. With them, it was a personal thing. Aloofness would probably be a better description."

Julie went on. "All right, if we accept that he was an honest and dedicated public servant, which appears to be the case, he would want to protect his find for the Egyptian government. He seems to have been very loyal. That may not mean much, because the prospect of riches can turn people into traitors. If he was patriotic, and afraid that something might happen to him, he would take pains to make a detailed record of his discovery."

"Agreed," I commented.

"So he did," Joe said, "and someone murdered him for it. If that's so, the secret died with him and only the murderer has it, and we're lost."

"Not so fast!" Julie countered.

Joe went on. "Why not? If someone got his secret, they'd want to remove him so he couldn't give his secret to anyone else, or start the police on somebody's trail. Brilliant, huh?"

"Sure," Julie answered. "But maybe he wasn't done yet..."

Joe gasped. "This is going to go on forever, and I'm hungry. Can't you get to the point?"

"Joe," I cautioned, "never try to hurry a brilliant woman, especially when she's just about to pounce on the answer to our problems. If we don't go down to the dining room now, we're going to miss dinner. And at Club Med that would be a major catastrophe."

For Joe, that settled the matter. "Let's go."

I said to Julie: "This is with your permission, of course. Can you hold on to your train of thought through a massive dinner?"

She grinned. "It's a chance we have to take."

EIGHTEEN

Joe piled his plate high: veal medallions, roast beef, broiled chicken, ribs, new potatoes, peas, carrots, rice, macaroni and cheese.

"Chuck wagons were never like this!" he said.

We found a secluded table, set down our food, and went to the salad table.

Finally facing his mountain of gourmet victuals, Joe smiled and said: "These French have mastered the art of food better than anyone. I'm not talking for fifteen minutes."

"Want to bet?" I chided him, then turned to Julie. "Let's hear the rest of your theory."

Joe: "That isn't fair! She's got a plate of Club Med masterpieces in front of her, and you ask for a lecture."

"My dear Mister Muck," I said with a grin, "you forget the other facets of French cuisine. Meals are social occasions. They should take an hour or two, not fifteen minutes. People here are sophisticated. They do not wolf down their food."

"I can't help it."

"Food should be mixed with stimulating conversation. N'est-ce pas? Didn't you learn that in Paris? Did Kelly send you there for nothing?"

Joe subsided. "C'est juste. Stimulate us, Julie...between bites, of course."

She chewed her food and gazed unseeing ahead, as though absent-minded. I could tell, however, that her mind, far from being absent, stirred with a muster of thoughts.

"Turki made a big discovery. This we get from what little has been pieced together. He must have been perfectly aware that his life would be in jeopardy if anyone ever got wind of it. Logical?"

"Logical," I replied.

"He must have had an obsession with spies. I'm getting the opinion that they are everywhere in Egypt. So if you felt you were surrounded by spies, what would you do?"

Joe answered: "Move to Tahiti."

I said to Julie: "I get your point...I think. Are you saying he would try to hide all evidence of his discovery?"

"With prying eyes all around," she said, "what would you do? What other choice is there? If someone else heard about it, or got hold of a map, anything at the site could be stolen overnight. The Lost Dutchman Mine syndrome."

I said: "I'm with you, so far. Which means he wrote down what he knew?"

Joe: "That would be foolish."

"Foolish?"

"Sure. It would double his problem. He'd have to protect not only his own backside but also whatever he wrote down."

"Not necessarily," I replied. "He might write in English, to keep the rank and file out of his affairs. Our search of the apartment, however, didn't turn up anything. Not even a map."

Joe pondered for a moment: "Well, English is not a secret language. I don't buy all of that. Maybe he wrote it in ancient Sumerian."

"That's not a secret language, either."

"It would be to thieves."

"Doesn't matter. Apparently whoever wanted his secret got it, map and all. A branding iron could have done the trick very well."

"If that is so," Julie went on, "and he is as smart as you say he is, then they wouldn't get *everything*."

Joe asked: "Huh? You speak with crooked tongue. What do you mean?"

"They didn't get his notebook."

"Why not?"

"They didn't ask for it. They didn't need it. Under torture, he may have told them all they needed to know. We're the only ones who need a notebook. Turki's dead. He can't tell us anything."

Joe stopped eating for a moment. He looked at me and then Julie. "Are you trying to say ..."

"That his notebook is still around somewhere."

"Not if it was in his apartment," I said quickly.

"Just a theory, mind you," she added. "Maybe a thin one." She looked at me. "You're sure you didn't find anything like a notebook, field sketches and the like, in his apartment?"

"Nothing."

"You looked under rugs? Chairs? Refrigerator?"

I smiled. "Someone else had already done that."

Joe scoffed. "First places thieves look."

"No notebook. In fact, Samaan said it wasn't likely Turki kept anything of value either at home or in his office."

"All right," Julie went on. "If that is so, there are several other possibilities..."

Joe: "Such as?"

"He buried it in the sand." She smiled when she said that.

I acknowledged her joke. "Let's go to the next one."

"He gave it to a friend."

I jumped on that. "It's an unlikely possibility, but I've had it in mind while interrogating Maybelle's archeologists. Sandy, maybe. It's hard to imagine Turki having a confidant, but it could be possible."

"Oh, come on," Joe said. "Do you think anyone in possession of a great archeological secret would give it to an archeologist?"

I answered: "Ask Julie."

Julie waited, a trace of frown on her brow. "I count it a strong possibility that he gave something to Maybelle...He didn't have many other friends."

I said: "Then you would have to explain why Maybelle hasn't given it to me."

Joe slapped the table. "She's the murderer."

I reminded him that every one of them could be the murderer.

He shook his head. "Do you think anyone in possession of Turki's secret would let you in on it? *Anyone* in on it?"

"This is a twisted situation, Joe. It's always possible."

Julie: "He sent a letter to a trusted friend..."

Joe: "If he had one. Seems very doubtful to me."

I commented that the possibility had occurred to me. "I had hoped by now that someone would have come forward. Turki seemed to like and trust Sandy Santano, and I probed this relationship a bit. But Sandy seems honest and forthright. That may make him suspect, being something of a confidant to Turki; the question is still open."

Julie: "He hid the map without telling anyone. Or he hid it and was about to tell someone. Or they got it out of him."

I was astonished at Julie's flood of reasoning. "You're carrying intrigue to the limit."

"Exploring every detail," she said.

"That's the ranger in you," I responded. "Keep going."

Julie's voice become authoritative. "I arrive now at my last and most likely possibility."

Joe perked up. "Wait until I've been to the dessert and cheese tables." He rose abruptly and left. Julie and I looked at each other, laughed, and rose to retrieve our desserts.

Joe returned with a plate of chocolate chiffon pie and canteloupe wedges, plus brie, camembert, and assorted Swiss cheeses. Julie admonished him: "When you get up and walk in your sleep tonight, don't fall into the Nile."

"Why not? I might find Turki's map."

"It's not there."

Joe scowled at her mischievously and dug into his dessert. We all ate in silence for a while, finished dessert, munched on cheeses, and began sipping tea.

I must confess that I was as anxious as Joe to hear what Julie had in mind. But it would also be unseemly to hurry her.

Finally, Joe couldn't take it any longer. "Okay, where is it?"

She looked at us both, smiling slightly. I rather thought that she enjoyed our twisting in the wind, waiting and wondering, on the verge of a momentous discovery.

"All right," she asked, "what about a safe deposit box?"

Joe and I froze in position, our eyes converging on Julie.

After a moment, I surrendered defeat. "In the annals of crime detection, there is often a procedure so obvious, so simple, that it is completely overlooked. I plead guilty. Julie, you're a genius. For some stupid reason, this never entered my mind, and I never brought it up with Samaan. I shall do so at once."

I sprang up and left, hearing Joe say to Julie: "He certainly moves fast on a fumble. Why didn't you mention this earlier?"

"I didn't think of it earlier."

"Nice recovery!"

I went to my apartment, picked up the satellite phone, and called Omar. By the time I got back to the table, Julie and Joe had finished their dessert.

"He said it will take a day or two," I told them. "They know which bank Turki used. Omar has to get official authorization from half a dozen people. I told him I don't want anyone going into that box—if there is one—without my being present."

"Okay," Julie said, "what's next?"

"I want you two to get back to Cairo and wait. The antiquities dealers may have already tried to contact you. We do have our own project to pursue. I have some other things to look into and should be back by late tomorrow. I'll be in touch as soon as I return."

"Look for us by the pool," Joe said.

NINETEEN

The Egyptian driver pulled the Land Rover up to the earthen wall and stopped in a cloud of dust. I got out and went toward a pile of very old bricks.

Gushing, effervescent as ever, Veronica Swain put down her brush and came forward, wiping the dust from her overalls with sweeping hands.

"Barry! Barry! Barry! This is wonderful! We were just saying this morning how much we hoped you'd get here..."

Tab came out of a tent, clad in khaki shorts and red baseball cap, shook hands, welcomed me, and said to Veronica: "No, sweetheart, it was yesterday we were saying that."

Veronica ignored him and took my hand. "Come let me show you. You were the one to ask if there was anything before the pharaohs. I remember that. Come look at this wall—."

I protested. "Veronica, you're very kind, and I want to see all your work. But right now I—well, I have to get back to Cairo by—."

Veronica did not listen. She tugged me over to an earthen wall they had just excavated. "See! Look at the quality of construction. Six thousand years ago, mind you..."

She launched into a detailed description of the architects, sculptors, and potters that preceded the times of the
pharaohs. So carried away did she get by her own oration
that Tab finally interrupted. "Wait, wait. Barry hasn't all
morning to listen to you prattle—."

"Oh!" she shrieked. "Prattle is it? Like hell! Is *that*
what you think of it? Barry, this bastard—."

Tab raised his voice, eyes flashing: "I'm just trying to
say that Barry didn't come out here for a lecture. He came
to give us news about Turki." Turning to me, he asked:
"Didn't you?"

"'Fraid not," I responded. "No answers, but I have some
tantalizing questions."

Veronica: "Well, let us hear them."

"Did Turki ever mention to you two that he was interested in wadis and ground water and oases, that sort of
thing?"

Tab scowled. "That son-of-a-bitch wasn't interested in
us, our work, or our theories. Result: no communication."

"When he talked to the group at Maybelle's, did he
ever allude to things he *wanted* done?"

"No."

"Any projects he thought ought to be accomplished?"

"No."

"Did you suspect he might be working on something
of his own? Something on the side?"

Veronica answered. "Suspect? We suspected him of *everything*. Anyone that sneaky could have been up to anything."

"By 'sneaky,' you mean..."

She rolled her eyes and thought a moment. "I always
had the feeling that he was aloof...holding something from
us. Considered us peons. Know what I mean?"

"Guarding a secret, maybe?"

"Could have been. I wouldn't have been surprised.
Why? Are you on to something?"

"Only that he was interested in hydrologic studies. I found the books in his apartment."

She frowned. "That's something to get murdered for?"

"Depends. Have you two got anything along that line?"

"We did a little work on water sources near Saqqara, an area occupied just prior to the first dynasty. Djoser, you know, built the first big pyramid at Saqqara and—."

Tab: "Dr. Ross knows perfectly well who Djoser was. Don't insult him."

"I was just trying to... Oh, forget it. We have no way of knowing whether Turki ever read the paragraphs we wrote."

Tab interrupted. "Wait! I do remember. One time when he talked to Sandy Santano I happened to be nearby. He asked whether the drawings Sandy was photographing ever showed the lives of lesser figures than the pharaohs."

"Lesser figures? Are you certain?" I did not mention that I had discussed this with Sandy. I wanted their independent angle.

"Positive. I wondered at the time, because we always focus on the pharaohs, but the pharaohs had on their staffs some very important architects, painters, bookkeepers, concubines—."

Veronica snorted. "Keep it clean. Barry is referring to the ship of state, not a whorehouse."

Tab turned on her. "My dear ignorant sweetheart, if you don't think sex has ruled the rulers of history, then—."

"Oh, stop it. If you're going to get sentimental, you're not a fit scientist."

"Are you insinuating that—."

I had to interrupt this. "Wait! Wait! I must ask you both: have you ever been followed or contacted by anyone wanting to know *your* secrets? Results of your excavations? Things like that?"

It was something of a compulsive question. I'd had it in mind to make this inquiry somewhere along the line and decided suddenly that, peripatetic as the Swains were, this would be a good place to start.

Veronica was straightforward. "Sure, all the time."

I was astonished. It was the first time anyone had mentioned to me that archeologists were, in a sense, constantly followed. Stalked.

"We live with it," Tab added.

"By we, you mean Maybelle's group?"

"Sure."

I asked if anyone in particular had bothered them.

"Yeah," Tab answered without hesitation. "A little fat-ass we named Apis after the ancient bull."

"Where did you see him?"

"Cairo."

"When?"

"Frequently."

"Who else has been followed?"

Veronica tried to think. "Hami mentioned it, Mei Hua, Sandy…"

Not one of these had mentioned this to me, but I didn't say so. I was puzzled. Why hadn't they? Was it because I hadn't asked? Did they think it irrelevant, or unimportant? "What do they want?"

"In a word," Veronica answered, "antiki. They want to know where to get ancient things to sell. They know we dig. Discover things. They're little entrepreneurs. They sell anything. Even it it's obviously fake. Even if you can't tell whether it's genuine or not."

"They make a living at this?"

"Little statues bring big bucks on the black market."

"To whom do they sell it?"

"Direct to tourists," she answered in a very knowledgeable way. "Sub rosa. Or they give it to the boss."

This brought me full round. "Boss? You mean a syndicate?"

"What else?"

"Know any?"

With this she smiled, and shook her head. "My expertise doesn't go any farther than that, Barry. I'm an archeologist."

I went on. "Do you know if anything has been stolen from anyone, like maps and notebooks?"

"Not that we know of," Veronica replied.

"Any threats?"

"No."

"Offers of money for information?"

"Sure."

"By whom?"

"Anubis, Hathor, Zebek...Little Apis. They're not bashful. Quite open, actually. But I don't think you could get anything out of them. Or on them."

I asked where I could find them.

Tab answered: "Just stay around. And stay alert. This is Egypt. You'll have one of these guys in your back pocket before you know it."

"A syndicate?"

"Probably."

"Turki knew about them?"

"Probably."

"Where can I meet one of them?"

"Go down on the docks at Cairo. There's a little dilapidated brown house not far from the Papyrus Museum. I give five minutes for one of them to see you. Apis will find you before you find him."

They started arguing again. I excused myself, but neither heard. Stepping backward as their exchange heated, I returned to the Land Rover.

Veronica broke away from the argument and ran to me. "I'm sorry," she said, "we haven't been very much help to you."

"Oh, but you have," I answered politely. "And I appreciate it. You've told me that Turki was secretive, and in a public position like this, he shouldn't have been."

"A real bastard," said Tab, coming up.

"And you've told me he was interested in people around the pharaohs. I can't figure out all the connections yet, but I'm just beginning. And the stuff about little Apis and his world. I'm not quite sure what to make of that yet."

Veronica shook my hand. "Barry, they're having a mansef over in the village tonight and have invited us. It's quite an honor. Wouldn't you like to come? You can dine on goats' eyes and—."

Tab pulled her away gently. "My dear, he's not the least interested in eating sheeps' eyes…"

She turned to him. "How do you know what he's interested in? Did you ask him? Did you? I get sick and tired of—."

I signaled the driver, and the Land Rover went down the road in a cloud of dust.

TWENTY

I went away more confused and mystified than ever. Of all I've interviewed, only the Swains acknowledged so openly that archeologists are followed. Are the others concealing something? I thought I was on track, but not now.

This is a new element. I've been thrown off base. Maybelle's mob either doesn't know anything or they're purposefully vague. If I could only find this guy called Apis I might get something definite on Turki's murder. In a city of millions I must find one shady character?

Come on, stupid. Be realistic. You think you'd get something definite from dealers in illegal antiki? Indefinite is more likely, and you know it.

Well, at least I'd been given a start...I had a name and a place to look for the guy.

And then it came to me like a bolt. If Apis were part of a syndicate, I might also get a lead on the tomb robbers I was looking for.

On the way back to Cairo, I had an impulse. Why not try to find Apis now? I was due to meet Maybelle within the hour. I got out the phone and called her, saying I'd be a little late. She understood. She always understood.

I conveyed to the driver my desire to divert to the docks. Reaching into my bag, I pulled out a tie. If I'm to stand out and look wealthy, a tie would help.

The driver parked in a pretty dilapidated riverside location. I got out.

For five minutes, I watched a felucca being loaded. Nylon bags in blue, green and red went aboard. Backpacks. I speculated the sailboat was being used to transport a group of young people doing Egypt the relaxed way.

Maybe this was another goose chase. I didn't know whether or not to trust the Swains. Beneath their veneer of domestic strife they seemed like sincere scientists. Maybelle felt that way. How was I to know whether Apis would be here today? Or ever? They said five minutes. It could take hours.

And then surprise! At the end of five minutes, I'm approached by a short guy in a blue turban and white caftan.

"Antiki? Antiki?" he said, in a sing-song nasal tone.

I asked for Apis, Anubis, Zebec, letting a five dollar bill flutter from my fingers. I didn't have to do that, but it always helps. I had no idea who this little guy was. His eyes brightened, and his dark brown cheeks puffed out in a giggling smile. His fingers told me he thought he ought to have twenty dollars for a job as big and important as this, not a piddling five. I haggled by sign language for a while, and in the end wound up forking over a twenty dollar bill. He was a tenacious bargainer, but I secretly wanted him to win. If this led me where I wanted to go, it would be cheap at almost any price.

That's when I got taken to the dilapidated little building.

The man behind the desk, pasty-faced, high forehead, wavy hair falling down his back to a knot at the shoulder blades, glared with black eyes that seemed to have no finite depth. He picked up a rawhide quirt and snapped it across the little man's forehead, resulting in a line that began to bleed. The little guy recoiled and left, pulling out a rag to blot the wound.

That was brutal. If that was meant to show me who bossed this place and how tough he could be, it worked. He told me his name was Zebec, but that's all he told me. I didn't have to ask for his biography. I didn't need it. The more I got into this, the more I felt that I was falling into a black hole, tumbling into a bunch of faceless no-names selling "antiki."

Zebec sat back in his creaking chair, looked me over, and spoke a passable English. "You look for antiques?"

I followed his guttural tones with a low voice of my own. "Only the best. And I don't waste time."

He drew from his desk an alabaster statuette touched with gold, green and red. "Something like this?"

He offered the piece to me, and I took it, rolling it over in my hands and whistled so softly that he couldn't hear. It was exquisite, and I thought it authentic, but I didn't want to say so. I wanted to probe further.

"Fair quality. What dynasty?"

"Amenembek the Fourth."

That was an insult. There was no such dynasty and I knew it. But his indiscretion gave me the opening I wanted. "All right, if you're going to bring up a fake dynasty, this must be a fake piece made last week in some black hole in Cairo. If you're not going to be honest with me I will just get the shit out of here and try some place else."

Zebec's eyes narrowed to slits, and his scowl proved that I had angered the hell out of him. He picked up the quirt and slapped it down on the desk. Just let him try to slap it across *my* face...

Then he smiled. "I always want to know if my clients are serious. How about Amenemhet I?"

"How do you know?"

"Friend in university make identification."

I let him wait a few seconds, then nodded. "That's better."

"We have more."

"How much more?"

"A lot."

"Show me."

"Come back tomorrow."

I took great care not to ask the price. That was to let him know that price was no obstacle, but also that I had a good idea what these things were worth (which I didn't) and that he wouldn't get away with overcharging.

I wasn't ready to close the conversation yet. "Tomorrow I may not be here. Where is the rest of it? I'm ready to go there now."

He shook his head. "Oh, no, that would not be hospitality of Egypt. Mohammed will bring the mountain to you."

"When?"

"I can only ask Allah. Have you a card? A hotel?"

I looked at him for a long moment. "I'll be back. But only once more. If I don't see the rest of this then..." I trailed off, got up, and left.

He rose as I left the room, but said no more. I had cut off the conversation before he was finished. That angered him, but who was I to care? That was exactly what I intended.

Outside, I saw the little guy in the blue turban still wiping the wound on his forehead. I saluted him as I went by.

TWENTY ONE

On the way to Maybelle's I phoned Julie and Joe at
Club Med. As soon as Joe came on the line I ordered him to
switch on the scrambler.

"What's up?" he asked.

"I think we're onto something," I replied. I told him
about the leads from the Swains, my trip to the docks, and
the conversation with Zebec. "I think this is the guy we're
after. But I didn't go too deeply because I don't want to
interfere with your involvement. What I did learn was that
he doesn't have any stuff here, and he can't get it very fast.
He stalled me. This could well be the syndicate we're after."

"What's your next step?"

"If I can find Turki's notebook and get a map, I'm going out to the tombs."

Joe answered abruptly: "Are you mad?"

I said: "Coming up to Maybelle's. Call you later," and
powered off.

The Land Rover drove up the "tunnel entrance" of giant fig trees. Maybelle saw me from the garden and shouted:
"Wait there. I'll be right over." She put down her tools,
took off her apron, and came up, hugging me warmly.

"Barry, I've not seen you, you know, since that dreadful evening. Have you found anything out, yet? About Turki's murder, I mean?" She steered me to the huge door.

"Well," I answered without committing myself, "yes and no. At least not enough to convict anyone."

"Are you on the track?"

'Yes, I am."

"You know who did it, then?"

"I think so, but nothing is ever certain. Not even that."

She led the way through the foyer where Turki's bloody corpse had fallen that evening. "Andrea and I are having lunch. You're welcome to join us."

"Thank you, Maybelle. If only I could. I'll just stay a minute."

As we entered the dining room, my eyes fell on Andrea, voluptuous as ever, her eyes averted, her hands arranging the table flowers and adjusting the teapot.

"Hello," I said.

She lifted her eyes in the most sultry manner she could, and held out her hand. "Biscuit?" she asked, in a slowly rising tonal affectation.

I kissed her hand and took the biscuit, saying "Of course," and held the chair for her to sit. After Maybelle had spoken to the cook, I held the chair for her, too, then seated myself across from them.

"The cook is bringing a cup of tea," said Maybelle, "to go with your scone. Now you mustn't refuse it. I don't care how busy you are..."

"Oh, Maybelle," I responded, "thank you. It isn't that I'm so terribly busy...although I guess I'd better admit that...I am. It's just that I have an appointment."

"We understand," she said. "And I must confess that Andrea has been asking about you. You've made quite a stir in our little community, and Andrea has her eyes set on you."

"Maybelle!" Andrea said, seemingly embarrassed. "It isn't that at all."

"Well," said the elder woman, "I know a handsome man when I see one, too. I'd be making eyes at him if I were younger and you weren't here." She turned to me. "Have you your key?"

I grinned. "Maybelle, you should be ashamed. If I had a key to Andrea's apartment, do you think I'd tell anyone?"

Maybelle laughed. "I am ashamed. Of course you wouldn't. But I happen to know you have one. Andrea's very efficient... Now, how may we help you? What progress have you made?"

I answered in a forthright manner. "Very little, I fear. I've talked with Sandy, Hami, Mei Hua and the Swains... I haven't seen Ali Fawzi or Molly Holly, yet."

"The ones you talked to, they have motives?"

"Everyone has a motive. Except possibly Sandy. What I want to know—if you can tell me—is about any *future* projects Turki was interested in. Which leads me to ask something about how you manage your society. Who suggests the projects?"

"Oh, my!" said Maybelle, sampling her salad. "I have money, so I get very many suggestions. I always referred them to Turki. We couldn't get very far with any of them unless they were approved by the Egyptian government."

"Can you remember any of them?"

Maybelle thought a moment. "Well, yes. I do. Andrea, would you bring my notebook, please?" Andrea rose and left. "There was one chap from a chemical company who'd had some experience sealing sandstone and granite so that the rocks would hold together or erode more slowly. Like on highways. He wanted to try several processes under the Egyptian sun to show how they worked. His idea was eventually to coat the Sphinx and the Pyramids, even the Rameses statues at Abu Simbel, with some kind of protective layer."

"Was Turki interested?"

"Yes, but he had reservations. He said if we did that and the chemicals changed color under the sun, we would have a pink Sphinx. He knew that the rocks, especially those that make up the Pyramids, were not terribly durable, even though they have lasted five thousand years. They're limestone, and they do disintegrate, and something ought to be done. He was open to a test."

Andrea returned with the notebook. Junji came in with my tea. Andrea sat down, her eyes fixed on me. "Sugar?" she asked, her eyes black and masklike.

I replied: "Always." She dropped two lumps in my cup and let a trace of smile cross her face.

Maybelle leafed through her notebook. "Yes, here's a big company that wanted to take on nothing less than the complete restoration of the Pyramids, using the same limestone Chufu used. Turki was caught in a debate on that one. Some people saw no wrong in restoration—bringing back the real glory of the pharaohs. Others said we couldn't do it as well as the Egyptians had. Others called it a sacrilege."

"What about the search for tombs?"

She raised her hands in a sweeping gesture. "*Everyone* wanted to hunt for a tomb. We've seen dozens of secret maps—rejected them all."

"Why?"

"This was a sore point for Turki. He felt that if we hadn't the money to take care of tombs already opened, we shouldn't be trying to open new ones."

"Logical, don't you think?"

'Yes. I agreed with him. I honestly felt that he was right on that one, though he disappointed a lot of people."

"What else?"

"A naval expert proposed to study all the boats the Egyptians had, everything from papyrus rafts to the big ceremonial barges. Turki got interested in that. It was under serious consideration when he died. I could go on and on. Would you like to borrow my notebook and read it?"

I sipped my tea. "Well, why don't you keep it here and I will come back some time and look at it. In the meantime, I would appreciate any information on Turki that you can give me. And on the projects you sponsor..."

Maybelle rose. "I have files and clippings. I'll get them."

When she had gone, Andrea said, half in a whisper: "You've not responded to my invitation..."

I looked at her with eyes as soft as I could manage. "Tonight?"

"At nine?" she replied, coolly.

"That's all right," I said.

"For dinner?" she asked.

"I don't want to trouble you."

She lowered her eyes again and returned to her salad, saying softly: "I'll be waiting for you."

Maybelle returned. "This is a pretty bulky file, Barry, and rather disorganized, I'm afraid. I keep everything."

"That's good," I replied. "Sign of a brilliant mind."

"Oh, Barry," she said, flustered. "If you keep that up, I'll give you a key to my apartment."

I grinned, bussed her on the cheek, apologized for disrupting their lunch, and left.

TWENTY TWO

Leaving Maybelle's, I went directly to the bank to meet Omar Samaan. With all the approvals attained, he said, we could enter the vault with bank officials. After signing documents, of course, and agreeing to return all the contents to Turki's estate within two weeks. After that, we all went in to witness the opening.

Inside the box we found a gold watch, some jewelry, American dollars, and a notebook. I took custody of the notebook and directed that the watch, jewelry and currency remain locked in the box.

Thanking Omar, I went outside, got into the Land Rover, and began thumbing through the notebook as the driver took me to the hotel. The sun had begun to descend in the murky western sky, turning the pyramids on the plateau a light orange bronze. Putting the notebook in my backpack, I instructed the driver to let me out a dozen blocks early so that I could run to the hotel.

Once out, I loped down the narrow streets, past vendors' stalls and tables of merchandise, slipping in and out of the late afternoon shadows, making my way through clusters of pedestrians. I diverted onto side streets, circled blocks and markets, and resumed my course to the hotel, through congested sidewalks, past piles of giant baskets, and among intricate displays of fruits, vegetables and copper kettles.

Two kids came up and jogged beside me, shouting: "Pluma! Pluma!"

I stopped, pulled out two pens from my backpack, and gave them to the boys. They shouted with joy and ran away. I had learned long ago to keep a supply of pens handy if I ever needed help from kids. More than once it had worked like a miracle.

Within a block of the hotel, I heard a shot ring out. A bullet went past my head and zinged to the street stones with a sharp *whack!* From the trajectory, I could tell that the shot had come from above. Lurching to the side, I looked up and saw a dark unshaven face pointed down at me, the head encased in a red skull cap. I got only a glimpse before the head pulled back into a window and vanished.

I saw an open doorway and dashed inside. A single light bulb illuminated the interior. Upstairs I heard the frantic pounding of footsteps. From an opening in the second floor, metal steps descended to the ground floor. I darted up the steps, my feet clattering despite all I could do to tread lightly.

On the first landing I stopped. Only a dim light came from a window down the hall. The pounding of footsteps above had stopped. Since this appeared to be the only stairway down, the sniper must have taken refuge in a corner, or a vacant room, on an upper floor.

I slipped into a small alcove beneath the stairs to the next level, stopped and listened. Noises from the street filtered up from below. A radio issuing the mournful strains of an eastern chant came from somewhere within the building. Now and then, faint voices from a conversation drifted along the hall. The odors of cooking and the aroma of spices permeated the building.

I assumed the sniper was still upstairs, waiting to finish his work. He could have gone out some fire escape or back stairway, in which case I'd lost him. He probably was curious to know if he'd hit me or could still finish the job. Or the sniper could be starting down the stairs, aware that he had the upper hand in looking down and shooting at his quarry. I chose the first option, that the gunman remained upstairs. There had been no clatter of footsteps to this level, or the level above. Either the guy was scared, or, mortified at missing, intent on completing his task.

Drawing my 9mm Parabellum pistol, I drew back further into the shadows beneath the stairs. I listened. The sound of a footstep came from above.

I'd been right. The assassin, hearing nothing, would come down the stairs and, if his quarry could be found, try another shot. Depending, of course, on who saw whom first.

Another step. Then nothing. He had decided to use caution. He took another step, paused, and listened. He would be peering down the stairway, trying to detect any possible movement, his gun aimed and ready.

Aware of my disadvantage, I decided not to position myself for a look upward. I kept silent, moving not a millimeter. If I knew human nature right, the silence would draw the man down. One step at a time. I raised my weapon to a 45° angle.

Another step. Silence again. The little black guy might be hoping that his quarry had fled and could be shot some other time. If that were so—.

In the next four seconds, the man's rush down the stairs came so suddenly, so noisily, and with such a loud clatter, that it almost caught me off guard. The shadowy figure sailed past and headed on down the stairs.

Always reluctant to use my pistol in crowded surroundings, I held fire and raced down the stairs in hot pursuit. I saw him race out of the opening, moving so fast he miscalculated and hit the molding. This twisted him around and he almost fell, but got back on his feet and went out of sight.

I followed him through the door and out into the street. He turned right, headed along the building, jumped a fence, and fled into a park. Beneath palm trees and patches of bamboo, I risked losing him, so I closed in, and, being faster and more powerful, leaped on him like a grizzly bear on an elk.

I pinned the man's shoulders and arms so tightly to the ground that his gun could not be brought into play.

In this position, though, I was vulnerable to kicking and explosive movements. Seizing the right arm, I wrested the pistol away, and curled the man's arm behind the back, forcing out an instant cry of pain.

Within minutes, a policeman appeared on the scene. I turned over the prisoner, showed the officer my security card, and asked if he knew Omar Samaan. No response. The officer did not speak English. I slowly repeated the name. "O-mar Sa-ma-an?"

With this, the officer nodded his head. "Samaan! Samaan!"

By gestures, I instructed the officer to take the prisoner directly to Samaan, and when the officer understood, drew out my notebook and wrote a message.

> *Omar. This man tried to shoot me*
> *near my hotel. Can you find out who*
> *sent him?*
> *Barry*

I tore the page out of the notebook and pointed to it, saying: "Samaan. Samaan." The officer nodded, and took the note. I retrieved the sniper's pistol. The officer took it and led the prisoner away.

Putting my pistol back in my pack, I turned and loped out of the garden, back to the street, and to the hotel. Entering the room cautiously, as before, I saw the briefcase, newspaper, and deodorant in exactly the position I'd left them.

I put in a call to Joe and Julie at Club Med, and left a message for them to return the call. After a quick shower, I dried off in time to hear the phone ring.

"Joe?"

"Barry, what's up?

"I have the notebook from Turki Husseini's bank box."

"Great. Anything important in it?"

"Sure is."

"Come on out. We're about to go to dinner."

"Sorry. I have a dinner engagement."

"Who is she?"

"Someone you don't know. We'll get together first thing in the morning."

"What do you mean by 'first thing?'"

"Seven. Bring me a croissant. We'll meet in your room."

"We'll bring you a full breakfast. What's in the note-book?"

"See you in the morning. Have you heard anything?"

"Yes. We have contact."

"With whom?"

I fell into that trap without thinking—and Joe administered the coup de grâce. "See you in the morning."

TWENTY THREE

Withdrawing the key from its small envelope, I inserted it into the paneled door. With a slight nudge, the door swung slowly open. I stood there for a moment, looking in. A lone candle illuminated flowers on a small table, a sofa, a bookcase, a window and terrace looking out over the Nile.

I studied every element of the little room. Nothing moved. A door led off to the right. A faint light issued from the room beyond. Small pictures covered the walls, but in the darkness I could only identify them as copies of Egyptian paintings on papyrus.

I stepped in and closed the door. The light from the room to the right went out and the door opened. A lithesome figure emerged from the dark, carrying a tray with glasses. Without saying a word she glided barefoot across the tile floor and held the tray to me.

"Hello, Andrea," I said softly.

"Courtenay '56?" she asked.

I took the glass. As she moved closer to the candlelight, I noted that she wore a diaphanous chiffon gown that hung from the graceful curves of her breasts and the taut red upturned nipples. Her hair had been swept high and pinned with a comb of tortoise shell and silver. Her waist,

her thighs, her legs, all glistening, reflected the candlelight.
She wore nothing but oils, the gown, and the comb.

She walked in the darkness out on the terrace. I followed. Lights moved on the river. To either side, the lights
of Cairo fell back inland. A warm breeze lifted her body
veil and swirled it gently.

"I like the view," I said.

"Which one?" she asked.

"Well, Cairo," I answered. "It's brightly lighted. I can
see it better."

"Shall I turn up the candle?"

"Let's just watch for a while. You like Cairo?"

"Obviously. I always have."

"Always? You've been here a long time?"

"Yes. You've been here before?"

I answered: "Once. I like it, too. How big is Cairo?"

"You need a guide book."

"I have one. I'd rather hear you tell me."

She waited before answering, looking out to the lights
of the boats in the river. "Maybe twenty million."

"Many of them," I responded, "poor, hungry and home-
less. How can you live in all that? Isn't it depressing?"

She answered casually. "I don't see it."

Returning inside, she went through the side door and
switched on a light in the kitchen. I watched the Nile until
she had brought the dishes from the kitchen. She approached
from behind me, circled my waist with her arms, and whispered in my ear: "The table is waiting."

Asparagus, lettuce, a dash of *fool*, morceaux de poulet,
hot rolls and butter.

"I'm glad you served *fool*," I said. "I always like the
light taste of it. But you serve the beans with onions and
olives. You're different."

"I'm Spanish," she said softly, lifting a fork of chicken
to her lips and nibbling on it. "I have a great deal for you to
taste tonight."

I laughed inside, then asked her directly: "Did you
know Turki Husseini well?"

Her brows and eyelids lifted. "Are you still on duty, inspector?"

"I am always on duty. I am trying to find out more about him. Did he have a key?"

Her brow knitted in a frown and her eyes narrowed. When she spoke, there was acid in her voice. "Would you like a list?"

I went on, ignoring her question. "Most people I've talked to hated him. Did you?"

She ate for a while without answering, a sign that my queries offended her. I didn't care. I was assigned to solve this case, and that meant any where, any time, any person. She asked, her voice again soft and gentle. "Do you like Mozart?"

I registered no surprise. She did not want to talk about Turki Husseini. If this stymied me, there wasn't much I could do about it while a guest in her house. It was doubtful that persuasion would work. She was bent on sex, and that was that. I answered: "Mozart was one of the most gifted musicians of all time."

"Do you like him?" she repeated.

"Of course, I do."

She reached over to a cabinet beside the table and pressed a button. The strains of the clarinet concerto, second movement, filled the room. Sipping her wine, she said: "Why have you come to Cairo?"

I wondered how soon she would get to that. Did she really want to know? Or did her words retaliate for the bluntness of my questions?

"Why do I go anywhere?" I answered obliquely. "I am on the lookout for crime."

"Do you find it in Cairo?"

"I find it everywhere. I found it in the Amazon, and the murderer died."

She seemed suddenly curious. "Did you kill him?"

"I found a murderer in the Grand Canyon..."

"And did you kill him, too?"

Her persistence annoyed me, but I did not reveal it. "Do I look like a killer? Would you invite a killer to your table?"

"I'm very interested. Where else have you been?"

"China," I answered. "Argentina, Spain..."

"You have been to my country?"

"Yes."

"You like it?"

"I think it is one of the most wonderful countries on earth."

"And its people?"

"I love them all."

"You speak Spanish?"

"Cómo no," I replied. "Estuve en Cazorla varias veces."

We lapsed for a while into Spanish, discussing the places I had visited, the people I had met, the foods I had eaten...

She rose and cleared the dishes, returning from the kitchen with two cups of tea.

"You are fond of Maybelle?" I asked.

This time, she found no objection to my question. "Everybody loves Maybelle."

"Did she get along well with Turki?"

She sipped her tea. "Now you are a detective again. Why don't you ask her?"

"I'd rather hear it from you."

She smiled. "You used that line before. Do you wish to flatter me?"

"Of course."

She sat up, thrusting forward the transparent chiffon that clung to her breasts. "Well, then, what do you like about me?"

I didn't quite know which classic answer to apply to that, pondering it for a while before taking the simple route. "Everything."

She sat back and picked up her teacup. "I like that."

"But you won't answer my questions."

🐦🐦🐦🐦🐦🐦🐦🐦🐦🐦🐦🐦🐦🐦🐦🐦🐦🐦🐦🐦🐦🐦🐦🐦🐦🐦🐦🐦🐦🐦🐦🐦

"Well, you must understand that I work with May-belle. I cannot talk about things that relate to her. Or that take place in her house. Do you understand?"

I returned her question gently. "You are very loyal to her..."

She rose and went to the terrace again, a sign that she wearied of questions. She meant for me to follow, and I did. When I reached her, I saw that the chiffon veil had been discarded.

With a lithesome motion, she took my arm and lever-aged her body to a position directly behind, crushing her hips and torso against me, reaching her slender arms around me again.

We did not speak. She communicated with her arms and hands. She let her obviously well-experienced fingers walk up to my chest, feeling the hardness of my muscles, the tightness of my nipples. She caressed my shoulders and arms, lingered again at my chest, breathed softly into my ear.

Her fingers fell and grasped the hardness in my groin, then explored the hips, returning again to my crotch. Her breathing became more labored, her tongue reached out and slid along my neck and to my ear. She began to move her body, slowly increasing the rhythms. After a little of this her hands rose to the muscles of my abdomen, dug into them briefly, then dropped away entirely.

She withdrew from the terrace and opened another door. Inside, a candle burned beside a bed. She stood by the bed for a long moment, awaiting my arms to encircle her waist, rise to explore...

When that didn't happen, she sat on the bed, and slowly rolled over on her back. Her head took a position from which she could see the door, see me enter naked, as she imagined, step gently to the bed, look down at her, whisper softly about her beauty as she lay there. Then I would lay my heated torso on hers, our lips would meet, our hips would meet, and then...

I cannot imagine a more tempting seductress. She had everything a man could want...and many men had had. She was incredibly attractive. Her magnetism had an almost irresistible pull...if you liked that sort of thing.

Yet I was revolted by her, by the whole setup, the crass reduction of everything to animal lust. As though this were the most important human activity. Indeed, the fundamental purpose of life.

To animals, yes. To overheated, oversexed human beings, yes. I found her attractive, I liked her, and I considered her conversation stimulating. I wondered why she felt that she had to terminate our discussion and head for bed. Was she that much in heat?

Something more than her animal instincts bothered me. I had a sense of irritation that she had avoided every one of my questions, diverted my every effort to find out something about Turki Husseini. Sure, she was hot-headed, impulsive, a vixen, and very brilliant, as near as I could detect. Why then did she close down communication? Or maybe, she just wanted to communicate in other ways.

I thought of whole populations of wildlife across the world heading for extinction, and people pleading with me to help. To me, nothing else mattered. People wanted me yesterday on the Great Barrier Reef, where corals were dying. They wanted me here, where whole collections of antiquities were being stolen. I couldn't get all that out of my mind. I couldn't sully it by bedding down with a sex tiger. She had insulted what I stood for. She had insulted me.

I was tempted, but I would not yield to this debasement, however hospitable, however sophisticated. Neither could I hurt her if I could possibly help it. That was not my way. If she were only following normal instincts in a lonely world, I could only pity her.

I knew what I had to do. Withdraw as quietly as possible, try to let her gently down...

I lifted the flowers in the slender vase and laid them on the table. In their place, I left a single rose that I had brought, its color enriched by the flickering flame of the candle. Then I opened the door quietly and left.

As I waited in the hall for the elevator, I knew what was happening. She got up and came toward the table, her face a mask of rage, her eyes reflecting the candle flame as though mirroring a burst of cannon fire. I heard a shriek of fury. She seized the vase with the rose, opened the door, stepped into the hall, and hurled it at me. I ducked, and the vase struck a corner of tiled floor, where it clattered and broke into flying fragments.

She turned, entered the room, and slammed the door.

TWENTY FOUR

Joe and Julie carried breakfast for three to their little cramped room at Manial Palace Club Med, and waited for me. I arrived on time and immediately asked: "Who contacted you?"

Joe answered. "We don't know. A message to the Club desk. A car with the following license tag number would pick us up at Ezbekiya Gardens this afternoon between one and two."

"What else?"

"That's all. No special instructions. Nothing to bring. Just be there. Now tell us, what did you find?"

I pulled out Turki's notebook and took a sip of orange juice. "Julie was right as rain. Turki put all his secrets in here."

Joe: "Sum it up."

"No. I want you to read this just as he wrote it. And then we'll see if you come to the same conclusion I have."

"Read on."

"Let's give that honor to Julie." I handed her the notebook. "Read it aloud."

Before she began, Julie took a big bite of buttered biscuit, chewed and swallowed it, then a long swig of orange juice.

▼▼▼▼▼▼▼▼▼▼▼▼▼▼▼▼▼▼▼▼▼▼▼▼▼▼▼▼▼▼▼▼▼▼▼▼▼

"My discovery." She read Turki's words slowly, trying
to decipher his handwriting. "I make a record of this and
put it in my bank box for security. I am not to live long
because some peoples follows me and tries to steal my secret. Allah will guide and protect me, blessing be unto him.
But I know I not have long life yet."

She paused. "I pity the guy. He sounds scared."

Joe said: "He refers to 'some peoples.' That bothers
me. Sounds like a lot of goons were after him."

She continued reading. "I long had idea. I study all
about pharaohs in my university. Everybody study about
pharaohs. Know about mortuary temples. Know about
tombs. Dynasties. Many pharaoh tombs excavated now. But
I could not believe that nothing left. I think about all people
work for pharaohs. They had viziers, architects, scribes. I
know must be many people..."

Joe interrupted. "Vizier?"

I answered. "Head wrangler."

Joe grinned. "I get you."

Julie: "He lists some more." She read from Turki's notebook: "Generals of armies. I knew scribes very important in
history Egypt. Scribes write many things, stories of war.
Victories in battle. Laws of kings. And many praises of god-
king pharaohs. I go on to think these people sometimes
very much in pharaoh's favor. He like them. Reward them
for all their work. Give them gold necklaces. Give them
alabaster statuettes. Things of turquoise, faience, everything.
They became rich..."

Julie stopped. "I'm beginning to get an inkling of what
this guy was driving at. Sounds to me like a different con-
cept, a whole new field of Egyptian studies. Surely other
archeologists must have thought of this before..."

"Probably," I agreed, "but maybe never had time or
expertise to follow through."

Joe said: "Comes the dawn. He was after sites where
these people might be buried."

"That's what he says," Julie responded, going on: "Sometime I know these people buried with pharaoh to go with him on big journey. But then, I think, many times people fight. Try to get favor in front of pharaoh. Or maybe lose favor. Or pharaoh suddenly die, and these people have to hide to keep from getting killed..."

Joe said, with a smile: "The Democrats and the Republicans. Change of administration. Or any big business. People fall from favor, get removed with severance pay. Turki's one smart cookie. Why not? Why couldn't that have happened in ancient Egypt?"

I added: "We know it happened in ancient Greece and Rome."

Julie: "The Cleopatra legend?"

I said: "I got it from Plato. It comes under the heading of fluctuating fortunes. Go on."

Julie read. "So I think of English word *outcast*. What about some one who had to leave position and go to exile? I think he would take family, find place to hide, take all possessions, die there.

"Then I think, to hide some place, maybe go into desert, find cave, place of some spring water nearby, and live there. Maybe in wadi. And I think of wadis and go get some books on underground water systems in desert. Things not so dry in ancient times as now. More springs then. Desert not all dried up yet from Ice Age.

"So I read hydrology books. Try to find out about circulation of water under wadis, near oases. I look at air pictures of distribution of springs, wadis in desert.

"Find place where wadis come together. Look for place where maybe grass grows today, maybe site of spring long time ago. Family go there."

Joe interrupted. "Mighty neat reasoning, if you ask me. He figures the outcasts had a spring and a cave and retired there with all their goodies."

"Goods," I corrected.

"Yes, sir."

"Possessions," Julie said. "Wealth. Family jewels." She continued reading. "I find map, compare wadis and springs. Look up cliff that might have caves. So when I put all together, I find site very promising. So I decide not to drive there and leave tracks. I get helicopter pilot friend Amir to drop me nearby. I walk around cliffs, down walls of Wadi Faed, come to junction with Wadi Sostris, see place where spring water was and find cave. Small opening. Roll away big rock. Find tomb. Five mummies. Every kind of thing. Not big things like tomb of Tut-ankh-amun. Little things like gold, chests, statuettes, masks, jewels. I read inscriptions. This is tomb of scribe named Khostris, in Dynasty of Amenophis IV."

Joe let out a long slow whistle. "Aiyee-ee! This guy everybody hates came on a fabulous treasure."

"I'll say he did," said Julie. "Listen to this." She read from the notebook. "I find alabaster carvings of animals. Fifty of them, maybe with hieroglyphs I cannot yet translate. I find other tomb inside next cave, with little mummies. I have found a family. But I do not find hoes or seeds, which I think mean people had friends on Nile who bring them food. Clothing. Every thing. I find some baskets with dried up fruit. Also flutes. Mats. Fish bones..."

Julie stopped. Her eyes rose from the notebook, focusing on some distant celestial sphere. "Imagine the drama. They're exiles. Isolated in a desert, the government hostile to them, trying to raise a family, dependent on friends for food. They didn't dare go back to the Nile themselves. Where would they send their children? No playmates, nothing..."

She paused for a minute, and no one said anything. Then she continued in a low voice, a voice fraught with emotion.

"They must have lived so they could...could die..."

Joe: "What else does he say?"

She read: "Now I must be very careful. I must get someone to guard tombs until I can get team to photograph ev-

erything *in situ* and then we take all out to Cairo Museum.
I must number every piece and describe it, and show its
location. But someone has found out what I am doing. Of
course, I am always being followed because there are jack-
als who would take these discoveries away from me, away
from Egypt...and sell them. I am going out now to photograph the tombs. I must hurry."

Julie sat back. "There it ends."

Joe: "Nothing else?"

"There's a map. He appears to have pinpointed the location."

"Barry, did you find any negatives, prints?"

"No. He may have been trying to photograph in the
tombs when he was killed."

No one spoke for a minute, carried away with the stark
drama of this five-thousand-year-old tragedy, the excitement
of Turki's discovery, the suspense of thieves on his trail, his
own murder...

Joe broke the silence. "I can finish it for him. He went
out to get his photos. The robbers surprised him in the cave,
tortured him until he revealed the other cave, then killed
him. They took an inventory of their own, picked up a half
dozen pieces and left. They photographed these pieces, made
a brochure, and sent a copy to someone in New York. Juergen
Bigelow, got it, showed it to Kelly Ross..."

This peroration stunned Julie. She looked at him wide-
eyed.

"You think Turki's murder has a link to *us*? That we
are here to try to buy the things he found in those caves and
got murdered for?" Joe looked smug, saying nothing. "That's
fantastic!" she went on. "It's just too much."

They both turned to me. I said simply: "I figured
you'd reach the same conclusion I did."

Joe let out a whistle again. "That changes the whole
goddam focus of this thing."

"Not really," said Barry. "Kelly saw these as stolen
goods in the folder and got mad."

"So here we are, dropped smack into a murder case as a result."

"That's about it," Julie commented.

I offered: "Makes things rather simple, doesn't it?"

"Yeah," Joe answered. "We go break up a gang of thieves, get the murderer, and pick up the loot for the Cairo Museum."

"Treasure," Julie said.

"Treasure," Joe corrected himself. "Then we get shot."

I hated to break up their reverie, but I said: "We haven't much time."

Joe: "What's the plan?"

"You meet your contact. I'm going to try to get out to the tombs tonight and see if the contents have been disturbed."

"Aiyee-ee!" said Joe. "And what if they go there at the same time?"

"That's exactly what I want," I said. "Your meeting with them will almost guarantee it."

Joe shook his head. "Okay, so what do you do when you find them? Take on this gang of thugs single-handed?"

"If I must."

Julie said to me adamantly: "You're are not going out there without us."

"You have your own path to pursue. We'll mesh. But time is short. I have to get out there and stop them before they screw up the tombs."

Julie insisted: "You may as well get it out of your head that you're going out there alone. After they contact us, they'll be out there unloading the stuff tonight. Your friend Zebec said as much."

Joe: "We are not going to let you indulge in a suicide trip. You may remember that after the game with Las Vegas—and I've damn well told you this before—I was known as the best flying tackle in the Conference. That will come in mighty handy if we get close to these hoods. Otherwise, you are aware of my medals for marksmanship."

I frowned and closed my eyes. These two were impossible, impulsive...and heroes in my book. Neither of them would stop at any danger. I didn't want them to go. I loved them both and didn't want them to be wiped out by the syndicate before they'd even had their honeymoon. I didn't want them wiped out before or after their honeymoon. Especially not in a lonely wadi in the Egyptian desert.

With their minds made up this way, I could only stop them by canceling the whole trip. Then they would accuse me of running from it. Hadn't they been hired to help in everything I did? Weren't they two of the most loyal and enthusiastic people I'd ever found? It would kill them not to go.

I relented. "Next time I hire somebody, he or she is going to be a hell of a lot more obedient. Without argument."

Joe said: "He's breaking down."

I responded: "Oh, I've already decided to let you go. Now, if you can possibly listen carefully, and get the heroism bit out of your skulls, here's what we'll do. You go to your meeting. It will probably be the next step—showing you some more pieces and arranging for the transfer of funds. Don't pay them anything yet. Tell them you're tired of waiting, though, and if you don't get what you want on the next trip, you'll go back home."

"Roger. What will you do?"

"I'm going to Omar and a friend in the Egyptian air force and see if we can't get Turki's pilot, Amir, to fly us out to the site before dark. He knows where it is. We'll investigate the tombs, if we have time. Then we'll lie low and wait to see what happens."

"If anything," Joe cautioned.

"Where will we meet you?" Julie asked.

"I'll have dinner at seven with you here at the Club. After that, if all goes well, we take off."

TWENTY FIVE

Amir flew behind cliffs along the edge of the Wadi Faed. Approaching the junction with the Wadi Sostris, he circled to see, in the setting sun, whether anyone else was there. Finding no evidence, he settled down about a mile upstream from the junction, let out Julie, Joe and me, and flew away.

As the noise vanished, we found ourselves alone in the midst of the Egyptian desert, hugging the wall of a dry wash, looking from one end of the sky to the other for approaching aircraft, and one end of the wadi to the other for approaching vehicles.

The ultra-dry wash had the faint aroma of a dusty closet that had not been opened for generations. Of a haunted house that had not been occupied by living beings for ages. Sand and dust had blown in and settled between the white rocks in the ancient river bed, unwetted perhaps for years.

We saw no sign of anything else, no birds, no mammals, not even a scorpion. As near as we could tell, we were alone.

Joe watched the vanishing helicopter, then whispered: "It will be an hour before my hearing comes back."

I gave instructions: "Joe, you take the other side of the wadi. Julie, you stay behind me. I will head for the

junction. As soon as we get there, we'll reassemble and try
to find the entrance. It's going to be difficult, but I think
we'll have tracks to follow. If you hear anyone approaching,
freeze against the rock. You have on khaki clothing for cam-
ouflage."

As we crept along, I assessed the situation. The wadi,
with a bed of mostly white rocks mixed with sand, made
walking tricky, so that we had to watch where we placed
our feet. The old stream bed was about a hundred yards
wide, and since the sun had set behind the thirty-feet-high
cliffs on the western side, we were already plunged into the
shadows of evening.

The sky above, brown and dusty, further obscured the
illumination of our path, such as it was, so that we had to
be very careful lest we twist our feet in a cluster of rocks
and break a leg. We could barely see Joe on the opposite
side. Julie walked about thirty paces behind me.

On our side, the cliff rose almost sheer for thirty feet,
which meant that whenever we made an unavoidable clatter with our feet, the sound echoed from one side of the
wadi to the other.

That bothered me most. We had scouted this stream
bed for aircraft or motor vehicles, but what if some human
being, or a gang, waited behind rocks or within hidden clefts
for the arrival of intruders? I had no idea what Zebec's plans
were. The people with whom Julie and Joe met this afternoon merely confirmed that the two were still in the market for tomb treasures. But that could mean that the artifacts would be removed as soon as possible, and doubtless
at night.

I wanted to walk fast, even to run, but didn't dare.
Time lay on me like a granite statue of Rameses. We *had* to
hurry, but couldn't. It brought back the terror of a recur-
ring nightmare about a refuge that had to be reached before
imminent, utter disaster struck. Our legs in such a dream
grew weak, our pace slowed, and we realized that we would
never get there in time...

There was no way to avoid a tinge of despair. First, that the tombs had already been robbed, skeletons kicked aside, priceless art broken, furniture upset, valuable art work stolen. Second, that we would arrive in time, but get caught by arriving marauders and, not having an escape route, could not fend them off. If we could only find the caves, get inside, and at least photograph the contents, even if we couldn't fight off the robbers, we'd have made some progress. But what would it help if we were trapped and caught in a siege, dying of thirst and hunger in an ancient tomb?

Some of the most valuable information in an ancient tomb was the exact manner in which any room had been left. The placement of furniture, the arrangement of bodies at death, the customs of the owners five thousand years ago.

With such treasure of knowledge, we would not get trapped. If we had to, we would fight like the blazes. We had to get out alive.

I also had second thoughts about my plan. Should I have brought a platoon of soldiers to be placed on guard in front of the tombs? Seal the caves and wait for a competent team of Egyptian archeologists to enter? I opted instead to catch the intruders. It was a thin decision. It could be horribly wrong. But if we succeeded, then we would have stopped a syndicate and saved no telling how many *other* tombs.

There was no time for remorse. We would play it as I had laid it out for us.

The closer we got to the junction, the more slowly I went, and thus proceeded more quietly, with less clatter of stones.

The next task was to find the caves. We came to the junction soon enough, and looked around in the dimness. Actually, it turned out to be less difficult than I'd imagined, for at the four walls of the junction, only one corner had cliffs sufficient to contain caves.

At that point, there was some vegetation and huge rocks broken from the cliff above and fallen to the slope below. Among those rocks, it seemed to me, could be the only passage to a cave.

Motioning to Julie and Joe to catch up, I took another look up the wadis and at the vast expanse of orange sky overhead. No visible signs of any other human beings, no noise of approaching vehicles or aircraft. The rocks on the river bottom thinned out and in the sand I looked for tracks. There were plenty of them. As soon as Julie and Joe came up, I pointed to the tracks, still not uttering a word.

The tracks pointed to and from the cliff. With this, we had no further question about which way to proceed. I set the pace, walking as fast as prudent toward the fallen rocks and thorny vegetation that surrounded them. In places, the tracks became difficult to see, but with a little back-tracking now and then, we managed our way around the first of the head-high boulders into a cleft behind.

Finding the actual entrance proved toughest, and we almost lost the trail when the footprints disappeared as we climbed over a fallen slab of rock. On the other side, however, we picked up the trail again, and saw a narrow black opening dead ahead.

Stopping for a moment, I motioned for absolute silence. We strained our ears to detect any sound either miles away in the sky, miles up the wadis, or close by—within the cave.

Nothing. Drawing Joe and Julie close, I whispered that we were now about to trap ourselves within the cave, that caves are notoriously soundproof and that we might not be able to hear an approaching enemy. For that reason, I delegated Joe to remain at or near the entrance, to provide a warning if necessary. I had no idea how deep within the cliff we would have to travel, but guessed that if he hailed us we might be able to hear him and respond. If not, he would come dashing in to retrieve us, and we would all hightail it out of there, doing battle if we had to.

That done, Julie and I squeezed through the crevice, climbed up over a ledge, and into the pitch blackness of the

ancient cave. Switching on our flashlights, we found ourselves in a short gray passage with a dusty floor adorned
with footprints. That was the first violation: the discover-
ers had already wiped out any original tracks that might
have been made by the ancient occupants, removed any valuable clues that such tracks could have revealed about the
last moments of their lives.

There could be sentinels ahead, syndicate gunmen
guarding the treasure, waiting to obliterate anyone who
might try to steal it from *them*. We switched off our lights
and looked ahead and listened. No illumination of any kind.
No sound.

So far, so good. There appeared to be no one in the
tomb.

The silence beyond our footsteps was absolutely profound. A musty odor overwhelmed us. Small strings of dust
clung to the walls and ceiling, evidence perhaps of ambient
dust caught in spider webs. Even though the last occupants
could have rolled a rock in front of the entrance, making
the cleft in the rock difficult to find and access, the cave
could still be open to insects, mice, lizards, any animals
living in that far-off time of more abundant moisture in the
wadis. In fact, we noticed collections of bones here and there,
evidence I supposed of ancient bats. Or perhaps leftovers of
small animals the ancient Egyptians ate.

I felt as though we were walking into a vault of an
unknown world, an unknown century. I felt reluctant to
breathe, lest the moisture in our breaths contaminate the
tombs. Maybelle's people decried moisture from tourists
penetrating tombs and causing slabs of paintings to fall to
the floor. I could remember caves in Kentucky so delicate
with fragile formations that the public was excluded for
fear that the force of human breath would cause the feath-
ery formations to fall. Yet I could not imagine anything
more fragile than the exact setting in which the occupants
of these caves left their possessions. We watched every step
we made, every wall we touched in passing.

For a few moments, we bent over as the ceiling lowered, but then entered a larger chamber filled with ancient furniture. Julie gasped. I felt a profound jolt, but knew that we had no time to gape with awe.

Setting down our packs, we both drew out small cameras with built-in flash and popped them in all directions. That was the first contingency record. We could compare these pictures with the shots first made by Turki Husseini when he came in here. A comparison would tell us what had been moved, what had been stolen.

Astonishingly, there were some statues of gold and alabaster on a shelf to the right. The syndicate had not taken everything out. That good news was partly erased by the recollection of the statue shown to me by Zebec, and the artifacts displayed in the folder obtained by Kelly. This was the cave!

Seeing a side room, we stepped gingerly among dusty benches and tables, and entered a smaller chamber. Cameras went up to record the scene: floor mats, skeletons large and small, jewelry, urns...

Scarcely had we glimpsed all this when I heard a faint sound of Joe calling, then the wisp of a motor that suggested the approach of a helicopter. It sounded like it came from above, and very likely there were clefts in the rocks that provided some air into the depths of the cave.

We turned and retraced our steps as fast as we possibly could, which wasn't very fast at all. The nightmare...agonizing...terrifying...repeating itself. We had to watch every step, every low ceiling. As we approached the entrance, the sound of the chopper became louder.

By the time we clambered over the last ledge and down through the cleft, the machine was visible coming low up the wadi.

I took the lead and veered to the left, dashing across the smaller width of the Wadi Sostris, trying to avoid the acacia thorns that would have torn our clothes and bloodied our arms and faces.

Straining every muscle, we ran as fast as we could, without any attempt to be quiet. For now the sound of the approaching aircraft filled the canyons with an echoing and reverberating roar.

The machine had not yet come around the corner. If it had, we would have been exposed in the middle of the wadi, standing out like black rocks in a limestone quarry, and gunned down on the spot.

Seeing a small cluster of fallen boulders on the other side, I made for them as fast as I could move, a race against time as the roar of the chopper grew louder and almost deafening.

Julie and Joe, close on my heels, strained, lunged, stumbled, striving in the last dregs of daylight to avoid the rocks that would have tripped them and cast them down on a sharp bed of stones.

Racing with only seconds to spare, expecting the helicopter to burst around the edge of the cliff at any moment, its passengers catching sight of us, and machine gun slugs to ricochet in all directions, we staggered mightily.

The aircraft moved more slowly than I expected, or its distance up the Wadi Faed was greater than I had calculated. We reached the cluster of rocks and dived behind them for a full twenty seconds before the machine came around the edge of the cliff.

Recognizing it as soon as I saw it close up, I felt astonished. The machine was a late model Bell Long Ranger, which I had checked out at a military airfield near Baltimore less than a year ago and flown for certification.

Well! That very expensive machine told me at once that this syndicate was better heeled than I thought. Or else they had enough to lease a top-rate aircraft for their work.

It was a big machine, and I knew from that that there would be several people aboard intent on carrying back a cargo of treasure.

They hadn't seen us yet. The pilot set the machine down on a dusty patch, sand flying up all around, and turned off the engine. While the blades were slowing, lights came on inside. In a few moments the door opened. Men with flashlights leaped out. I strained to see who they were, but identifying strangers in silhouette with flashing red lights, is next to impossible.

At least I could tell that no one wore a uniform. It was not a military mission. I didn't think it would be. Not until after the four men gathered outside and flashed their lights from one to the other to a pile of backpacks carrying equipment being unloaded, did I conclude that it must be the syndicate.

If they had murdered Turki for his maps, then these were the people we were after.

TWENTY SIX

The leader barked out orders in a guttural voice, and the men began to put on backpacks.

We kept low, hidden scarcely twenty paces away.

I noticed that the pilot had no part in this operation; he remained in his seat aboard the aircraft.

As the four men hoisted on the empty backpacks, I had a chill of despair. They were going into the tombs to load up, move the artifacts from their original locations, jam them, however fragile, into the backpacks, and bring them out. Sheer desecration. It chilled my soul.

A voice said to me: *Go out shooting! Now! Mow the bastards down! Don't let them even get near that cave. They must not even touch one of those priceless objects!*

I almost did it, too. Almost shouted to Julie and Joe to draw their pistols and follow me into the midst of a pitched battle. But as soon as this plan was abruptly formulated, I abruptly terminated it.

Wait! said another voice. *You don't start a rock to rock battle in pitch blackness. The pilot would pull his helicopter out and fly back to Cairo. You'd be here all night. Get those guys back out of there, some other way. Pull them out of there before they fill their packs with gold and faience...*

I watched them cinch up the pack straps, close the pockets and otherwise get ready. Within a few moments, the leader barked an order and they went around the nose of the chopper, up into the rocks toward the tombs.

We had to move fast.

I raised into a crouch, certain that the pitch blackness would now conceal me. The pilot had turned off the chopper's lights. He remained inside, though. We could see the glow of a cigarette.

Without telling Julie and Joe, I hatched a plan within two seconds, and set it in motion as soon as the flashlights of the robbers reached the cave entrance.

Tapping Julie and Joe on the shoulders, I whispered to them to get up and follow me. Walking as quietly as possible, I circled around the tail of the helicopter, which had come to rest pointing up the Wadi Sostris. This way, I could get between the machine and the tombs.

As soon as that had been accomplished, I tapped Julie and Joe and pulled them down to a crouch beneath the tail. Then I walked toward the tombs.

I didn't take much care to be quiet, for I imagined the pilot half asleep by now and paying no attention to sounds out the door.

I turned on the actor inside. I would play the role of a robber finding something wrong and coming back. Turning, I lifted my backpack and started toward the still-open door of the aircraft, muttering some unintelligible epithets beneath my breath. This mumbling I tried to make sound something like the muttering I'd heard from the four men as they left the machine to go to the tombs.

I approached the chopper slapping at my pack, making deliberate noises, with no suggestion of trying to sneak aboard. That would have alerted the pilot more than anything.

It was a bold plan of deception and could go wrong at any moment. However, I guessed that the pilot was indifferent to the whole operation. Now, I reckoned, if he waked from a snooze, he wouldn't be able to tell whether I wore a baseball cap or a turban.

I stopped for a moment at the fuselage, banging my pack against the side as though to knock something loose that had become stuck.

Then I climbed aboard.

Just like that. From what I could see by the soft lights of the instrument panel, the pilot nodded sleepily in my direction, never in his mind imagining that there had been someone else out in these distant, lonely wadis. I dropped my own backpack on a seat, took out the 9mm Parabellum, grabbed the barrel and let the pilot have it across the back of the cranium.

He slumped. I opened the door and pushed him out.

Without a moment's delay, I called to Julie and Joe, climbed into the pilot's seat and started the engines. Julie and Joe scrambled in, grabbed seats, and fumbled for seat belts in the darkness. The pilot groaned on the rocks below.

"Close the doors!" I yelled.

As soon as I got the rotors up to speed, I pointed my pistol outside and fired into the air. As I did it, I doubted that I needed to, but I wanted to draw those men out of those tombs fast, to see where the shots came from, to see what was happening. The gunshots would add to the roar of the rising helicopter, and the demon in me wanted them to see what was happening.

Within moments, lights began to flash from the cave entrance to the tombs, at which point I lifted the Long Ranger and got up out of the way before the robbers could see the pilot lying on the ground, get out their pistols, and began firing.

Joe was the first to explode with wild laughter. "Ai-yee-ee!! Barry! God damn, I never saw such a maneuver in my whole life! What happened?"

Julie shouted: "What are you trying to do?"

Rising up in the darkness, flicking on the lights, and setting a course for Cairo, I relaxed for the first time in hours.

"It's sixty miles to the nearest settlement," I said, not without a burst of glee. "They can't see how to get out of there until sunrise, and then it will be too hot for them to travel by day."

Julie rebelled. "You're trying to kill them! I can't believe it!"

I answered: "Naw. I only wanted to pull them out of the caves. They'll be so busy now figuring how to get back to civilization and avoid getting caught that they'll forget about the tomb stuff."

Joe roared with laughter. "Brilliant, Barry! Damn brilliant!"

Julie: "It isn't, either! You can't just leave them out there to die of thirst and starvation! That's inhumane, even for tomb robbers. I'm aghast that you'd even think of it!"

Joe shouted: "This is war! They were ready to plow slugs into you down there. This is not the Grand Canyon. Those aren't tourists. How polite do you want to be? Till you get your head blown off?"

She felt chastised, but still said: "I'm just trying to be humane. I don't want to be like those guys."

I laughed aloud. "Wait. Wait. I have no intention of leaving them out there. Just a good scare throughout the night. Tomorrow morning I'll have Amir take some police out to round them up and drag them in. If we'd had a firefight back there, someone would have gotten hurt. And I didn't want that someone to be either of you. Get it?"

With that I climbed higher and held the course for Cairo. Julie joined Joe in laughter. They never stopped jabbering all the way back to the city on the Nile.

TWENTY SEVEN

Time was short now. The syndicate would be livid, ready to stop at nothing to empty the tombs. And to get us.

After breakfast I called Amir. He said that at dawn he had taken out to the tombs two policemen, who took the robbers and their pilot into custody.

I put in a call to Omar to thank him, only to find he had gone to southern Egypt to handle a Coptic church bombing in which twelve people had been killed the previous night. I tried to call the head of antiquities, the guy who had taken Turki's place, to get a guard on the cave in the Wadi Faed and prevent looting. Alas, the guy was in Greece.

Things were falling apart, and I had to figure out which crisis to handle first.

The syndicate bosses would not know yet how their mission had misfired. I went immediately to see Zebec and tell him I'd decided to go ahead with the purchase if I could see all the pieces.

He received me with indifference. Since he had not heard from the robbers, he could be worrying about what might have gone wrong. He had no pieces to show me, he said. Not yet. But it wouldn't be long. They are very beautiful pieces, you understand. Like nothing else in all Egypt.

I said I knew all that and I wanted some action. Was he going to get the pieces or not? Why was he stringing me along, stalling, bluffing? He changed the subject and became very vague.

Slapping the quirt on the desk, he said simply: "Come back tomorrow."

Outside, walking along the dock, I ran into the same little guy who had suffered Zebec's quirt the other day. I could identify him easily from the scar on his forehead. This time he did not approach me with the words "Antiki! Antiki!" He knew who I was.

He pointed to me and asked: "Ross?"

I nodded. I pointed to him and asked: "Apis?"

He nodded. I half suspected it, but I was still taken by surprise that he would approach me so boldly like this in broad daylight. He wanted to talk with me.

I had a gut feeling that we should not be seen talking to each other. Not within sight of the little shack. Zebec might even then be watching through a crack in the wall, to see where I was going.

I quickly motioned Apis to follow me so that we could get out of range.

Approaching the Papyrus Museum, he pulled me to two kegs beside a tree, where passersby could not see us.

Sitting on the kegs, we began to communicate. He knew no English, I knew no Arabic. I had a lot of experience, however, in wordless communication. I pulled out a note pad, and drew diagrams and stick figures and pictures when necessary. The result was that, slow though it may have been, we conveyed to each other exactly what we wanted.

I showed him my Egyptian honorary security badge. He hugged me—the Egyptians are some of the most friendly people I know. If this seemed a bit odd, considering that he belonged to the enemy camp, he soon let me know what was up.

"I like Egypt," he said, through gestures and sign language. "This is my country. I don't want the tombs to be robbed. I am helpless. Zebec will kill me. But I have information."

Here he paused, and I knew exactly why. I pulled a U.S. ten dollar bill from my pocket. He scowled and turned his head away. I produced a twenty-dollar bill. He shook his head. I reach in for a fifty-dollar bill. I always keep these in a lining of my pack because I have been through such impromptu negotiations before.

What he had to tell me, however, was worth more than anything I had shown him. By the frown and the expression of "maybe" on his face, I knew I was getting close. When I showed him a hundred-dollar bill he was all smiles. He reached for it, but I drew it back and wagged my finger, motioning him to spill what he knew first, and then I would give him the bill.

This disappointed him, but he yielded and began to jabber, point and gesture. I stopped him and drew a series of stick figures with one alone at the top, asking in effect who was the boss of the syndicate. Zebec?

"No, no!" he answered "Isis."

That told me absolutely nothing. I frowned. "Isis?"

He nodded vigorously. I got across to him that I wanted to know who Isis was. He became animated, shook his head vigorously, and gave me to understand that he didn't have any idea, that *noboby* knew who Isis was.

I looked incredulous, overemphasizing my facial contortions for effect. "Nobody?"

He held up a finger and said: "Zebec."

So now I suddenly knew that Zebec was not the boss, but was the only connection they had *to* the boss. I repeated my question: "Who's Isis?"

The little man's eyes became fearful. He got across to me that Allah would strike him down if he ever revealed that. But anyway, he didn't know who Isis was, so he couldn't reveal it. With this he gave a little giggle, which I didn't find funny.

I frowned, getting across to him that I was paying a hundred dollars for information, and that was a lot of money, and I wasn't getting very much information.

"Is Isis in Cairo?" I asked.

He became fearful again, as though lightning were going to strike if he said any more. He shook his head vigorously, meaning: he didn't know.

At this point, impatient, I spread my hands in dismay and looked hopelessly and angrily up at the sky. As Stanislavsky said to actors: *Improvise!*

Apis wagged his finger, imploring me not to be in such a hurry. He took my pen and drew on my note pad a primitive picture of a big ship with airplanes flying about, which I interpreted to be a carrier. Then a map, showing the ship not far off the northern coast of Egypt, in the Mediterranean.

He now had my attention.

Indeed, I was suddenly intrigued, because I knew how U.S. military installations were so vulnerable to terrorist attack in the Middle East. Any connection, even voiced by a little fat-ass, as the Swains called him, could be serious. But how could he possibly connect that with Isis? Or Zebec? Or anyone?

He drew a picture of a felucca, and swept his hand downstream along the river. Then he drew a lot of little squares piled one on top the other. With that, he lifted his hands in a sudden gesture to the sky, saying: *"BOOM!"*

Explosives! Loaded on a felucca.

The skin began to crawl on the back of my neck.

A wavy motion of his hands. Pointing down the Nile. Then waving far to the north. Then he pointed to the picture of the carrier.

They were going to take a felucca, filled with explosives, down the Nile and go up to the carrier...and what then?

This time he jumped up and flailed his arms in a really wide sweep toward the sky.

"BOOM!"

TWENTY EIGHT

I sat absolutely stunned.

I could not imagine a more bold, hideous, deadly proposal than that.

In any other part of the world I would have thought it absurd for anyone to think of getting close enough to an aircraft carrier to blow it up. Not here. Whole barracks full of soldiers have been brought down by mere trucks laden with explosives. In this case, the "barracks," if damaged badly enough, would sink to the bottom of the sea.

A felucca could be a pretty big sailboat. How did I know from what distance a felucca laden with explosives could damage a naval vessel?

Now, they—whoever "they" were—had filled a felucca with, well, with what? Fertilizer and nitrate?

I asked Apis. He shrugged.

Filled the felucca?

Almost.

How much greater quantity of explosive could you get on a felucca than on a truck...? Enough to damage a vessel badly. I didn't need any more details.

I stopped thinking of it. You could just about cause fatal damage to anything on earth if you got close enough.

And who would ever think of an innocent felucca as a deadly weapon? Apis had an answer.

The Black Robe Terrorist Group. Yes, I'd heard of them. I got across to him that this job was too big and expensive for them. Who was this really being done for? Who hired them? Who paid them?

Shrug after shrug of the shoulders.

I asked what this had to do with the syndicate. It took a while for Apis to get the answer across to me, probably because it was so unbelievable, but I perceived when he finished that it was a simple transaction. The syndicate would sell the tomb statues, pay for the explosives, load the felucca, turn it over to suicide boatmen…and get handsomely reimbursed.

"If the carrier sinks," Apis added, "we get lots more money."

From where? I tried again. From whom?

Apis simply did not know what country this was coming from.

I wasn't surprised. He was a low man on the totem pole. The surprise was that he knew this much. And if you don't sell the statues? I asked.

He responded that they will sell the statues. Also, they have good credit.

That was a chilling statement. They would go ahead and do this whether the artifacts were sold or not.

Had they started already?

Apis gave signs of getting impatient with this conversation, if not fearful of being seen talking to me. Very big questions remained. I still wanted to know who Isis was. No answer. Which felucca had been loaded with explosives? Shrug of shoulders. Above all, when would this all take place?

The little man shrugged, pointed to the sun, got up, and left.

TWENTY NINE

That left me nowhere. Both in place and time.

Exactly nowhere.

I had all this urgent information, and there wasn't a thing I could do with it. The whole thing was so fantastic, I couldn't inform anyone else about it until I had some solid details. I had no idea how reliable Apis was, although I believed him.

I didn't, however, believe him enough to alert the Egyptian government or the United States Navy. Until I knew where things stood, I couldn't act. The felucca could be taking off right this minute... But I had to prove it.

Meanwhile, the tombs were sitting out in the desert unguarded. That was my first priority. I knew exactly where *that* project stood. One fumble, and I could screw that up beautifully. If I didn't get someone out there to guard the cave entrance, and fast, Zebec would be out there again, sneaking in and retrieving the treasures I was supposed to protect.

Riding back to the hotel, I got a call from Della. Mño had been shot and killed at Angel Falls and Sam Petrie wanted me to get to Venezuela as soon as possible. Dr. Brasher had called from Cairns to say the Great Barrier Reef was in serious danger and they needed me yesterday, and if I didn't get there pretty soon—.

"Thank you, Della. I'll take Australia first. Tell that to Sam and Brasher. Would you get up three tickets from Cairo to Singapore to Cairns and have them at the airport here by tomorrow?"

"You'll be finished in Egypt by then?" she asked.

"Things are getting worse by the minute. How've you been?"

"Fine, and you?"

"Great, Della. Ciao."

My mind whirled with Apis's revelations. I was hopelessly trapped. There was no use in putting out an all points call to board every felucca in Cairo and find the one laden with explosives. The martyrs would blow up the Cairo waterfront if nothing else. I had to find out which felucca had been earmarked for a death cruise and let it get out into the Nile before we slammed a missile into it.

We? I needed help. The unguarded tombs burned a hole in my mind. The next job was to find out where to get help. Maybe from the Navy. It was a long shot. But I was used to banking on long shots.

Then, surprise! At the hotel, I ran into the Swains.

"Barry!" Veronica gushed. "Praise Allah! We've found you."

"What's up?" I asked.

They took me by the arm and led me into the restaurant. Over a cup of tea they made their momentous announcement.

"We had a meeting," Tab said. "All of Maybelle's mob. They decided they were going to help. It was unfair for you to shoulder this burden of Turki's murder alone. It's not just your job. It's our job. All of us. All of Egypt. We've got to find out why he was killed and who did it, and stop this kind of stuff."

"We know why he was murdered," I said.

That visibly shook them. They looked at each other with wide eyes. "Why?"

"Tell the archeologists that I deeply appreciate and admire what they have done. Tell them also that they are not trained investigators. This is a very dangerous case, and I do not want to endanger them. Time is very short. I have six problems in my lap and they could blow up at any moment. Literally."

Veronica held up her hand. "I knew it. That's why we want in on this. Which problems shall we take?"

Tab added: "We are not going to accept any nonsense, Barry. You have been overruled on this. Surely there are some things we can take care of and leave all the bang-bang-shoot-em-up to you."

"I won't have it." As soon as I said that, I suddenly realized that maybe he had a valid point. I didn't want them underfoot. If I could sick them off on some wild tangent, they wouldn't interfere with what I had to do.

"You can't stop it," Tab said. "You might as well be reasonable and bring us into this."

"I won't."

"If you don't, we'll start boring into this thing ourselves. That'll screw you up more than anything else."

"You don't know where to begin."

"That won't stop us. We'll find out. The mob is absolutely determined about this. You saw them. You met them. They're a bunch of stubborn characters and you know it. You ain't gonna stop them."

"Who's behind this?"

"Sandy, Hami, Ali, Molly, Mei Hua, and us. That ought to scare you!"

"It sure as hell does. What about Maybelle?"

"She doesn't know anything about this. She'd only disapprove it."

"Well, there's one sensible head. I told you this was dangerous, and now I know that it is more so than I thought. Deadly, in fact. And I'm not surprised."

"How? What do you mean?"

"Never mind. The whole idea is absurd."

"Where's your friend Samaan."

"In the south."

Veronica squealed. "You see? You can't go on with this alone."

I stopped and thought it over again. This wasn't going to quit or go away. I could see that. The last thing I wanted was a bunch of high-grade, hot-headed scientists diving off into deep water. They could botch up everything I'd been trying to set up.

They didn't know about the tombs Turki had discovered. They didn't know about Zebec and the syndicate. At least, I didn't think they knew. They didn't know who Isis was, the master mind. Or maybe they did. The situation was confusing enough without all this complication.

On the other hand, they were all pretty intelligent people. But if I sent them off in different directions, they could flounder all over the place, stumble into danger, and interfere with what I was trying to do. When I finished arguing with myself on this, I decided that it would probably be better to put them to work. My only hope was to get them out of the way long enough to choose my own path.

"All right," I said. "I give up. You win. But I want it clearly understood that I am in charge of this investigation, and if I give somebody something to do, I want it done according to specific instructions. Is that clear?"

Veronica looked at Tab, stunned by the quick turn of events. Then back at me: "Why, of course it is. Nobody doubts you're in charge. They want to help. They just want instructions."

"All right, then, I'll give them to you."

I brought them up to date about Turki's discovery, and I thought for a moment that they were going to fall off their chairs. More astonishing, they were speechless for all of twenty seconds.

Tab said: "How in the hell did you find all that out?"

"Because he's smart and you're not, you dumb ass," Veronica said.

"Never mind," I responded. "The first priority is to get that tomb sealed and guarded. Omar's gone, and the

head of antiquities is in Greece. I don't want to trust this to
anyone else. I'm going to see if I can get some American
military help."

"American?" Veronica exclaimed. "Bully for you,
Barry!"

"I do not, repeat, do not for a minute expect success."

Veronica's face fell. "Stop being so negative!"

I told them to get out a notebook. An archeologist is
never without a notebook. They did. "Now write this down
carefully. I'll be depending on you to transmit these instructions without error. Okay?"

"Okay," Tab answered, getting out an old, battered,
aluminum-bound field notebook.

"Tell Hami to look up anything he can find about syndicates in Cairo. The names I've run into are Zebec and
Apis, but those have to be false names. Have him do what
he can. Tell Ali Fawzi to plead with someone in Turki's
office for help in guarding the newly discovered tomb.

"I'll try to get some temporary U.S. military help. It's
going to be tough, because things are destabilizing here
and there, like the militant bombings in the south. But tell
him to keep at it. Ask Molly and Mei Hua to trace down an
underworld character named Isis. This person, according to
Apis, is the head of the syndicate, and may be responsible
for other tomb robberies. I want this whole thing stopped,
and it can't be done without snagging the top brass. Clear?"

"Clear."

"Try to get Sandy to take all his equipment to the new
tombs and make a complete record, trying not to touch anything. This will be tough. You'll have to get a helicopter
pilot named Amir to take him out there. I'll pay all costs if
the Egyptian government can't or won't. I want full visual
and digital records. Then he can go on back to Thebes and
finish his work."

"What about us?"

This was my toughest part. If I didn't give them the
most important task, they would be miffed. "All right," I
said, "you get the most dangerous part."

Veronica clapped her hands. "Oh, goody!"

I told them about Apis's revelations, that somewhere on the waterfront was a felucca loaded with high explosives. I wanted to know which felucca it was, what kind of explosives it had on board, when it was scheduled to sail, and where it was going."

"That's impossible," Tab said, in a wilted voice. "No one talks in Egypt. Not about things like *that*. Jesus, man!"

"Apis did. But I don't want you to go around asking a lot of questions. Just observe. Do you get me?"

"Yes. But we can't answer many of those questions by just observing."

"Do the best you can. And make this quick. See if you notice any felucca with a big hidden, tied-up cargo, and make a note on any distinguishing characteristics. When it takes off, we have to follow it down the Nile…"

"How?"

"I don't know. Get out the maps. Have you been out on the delta?"

"Sure."

"Check out the roads closest to the Nile. My plan is to keep track of that felucca, follow its progress. You got your Land Rover?"

"Yes."

"I'm assuming they will sail down the Nile and out into the Mediterranean. In this country there isn't much other choice. My job is to get in touch with the Navy."

"How will you do that?"

"Never mind. If you have any messages, leave them at my hotel. You have a cell phone?"

"Yes."

"Okay, we'll try to synchronize on that."

"Anything else?"

"Yes, my two assistants are here on a mission to buy the artifacts from the tomb and help trap the syndicate gang."

"Names?"

"Julie and Joe Muck. I'm going to call them now. But no one is to mention them. They are supposed to be innocent buyers with a lot of cash. I mention this to you because they may be involved very deeply in what happens. See you later."

They rose and rushed in great excitement out of the room.

I pulled out my phone and tried to call Julie and Joe. No answer. I tried the Club Med desk. *Les Mucks ne sont pas ici.* Lapsing into French, I asked where they'd gone. The response: some men came to see them, and they all went away together. What kind of men? I asked. One of them had long hair tied in a knot behind the back.

How long ago? An hour.

Dropping everything, I got out to Club Med as fast as I could. No Julie or Joe. Baggage still in their room. No notes. No phone messages. They had not had time to tell me—or anyone—where they were going.

I called Omar in southern Egypt. Nothing in the police log. Besides, Omar was so far from Cairo...

My worst fears had been realized. At first, I tried to tell myself that Julie and Joe had just gone to the little shack to make a down payment on the artifacts. Maybe it wasn't as ominous as I thought.

I was only kidding myself.

Zebec had Julie and Joe.

THIRTY

Everything was beginning to collapse around my ears. The tombs were open and vulnerable. Julie and Joe had disappeared. Maybelle's mob was on my back. And a boat loaded with explosives was heading for a carrier offshore. How did such a mess develop so suddenly? All I needed now was for Della to call and say that I was desperately needed in Outer Mongolia.

Deciding to go to the airport, I called the Swains to meet me there as soon as possible. I managed to get a military pilot to take us out to the carrier Atlantis, which Della had told me was stationed for a week just off Alexandria, on the northern coast. We radioed for permission to make a temporary landing on deck.

We flew down the Nile at my request, along the west branch to Rosetta. I told the Swains to get a good look at the river from the air and check out the roads they might have to follow if we later identified a felucca laden with explosives.

Tab and Veronica babbled and gushed with excitement as we left the coast and approached the giant vessel. Settling onto the flight deck, we were met by a lieutenant who saluted me and said: "Good morning, Dr. Ross. Applegate, sir. Captain Kane is waiting to see you."

The Egyptian helicopter took off to return to base. Veronica burst out: "What a fabulous place!"

"Lieutenant," I said, "is there someone who could take Mr. and Mrs. Swain around and show them the ship?"

"Yes, sir. I'll see to it. Will you come with me, please?"

The Swains veered off with another officer, after which the Lieutenant took me up to the captain's office.

Captain Reginald Kane, with a froglike but benign countenance and crewcut tinged with white, greeted me like a long lost friend. "How good to see you again, Barry."

I had a puzzled look on my face. "Well, likewise. Where did we meet?"

"It wasn't exactly a close encounter, but you came to the Academy to give us a briefing on international environmental law. Remember?"

"I certainly do. I always find it inspiring to meet with Navy personnel."

"You inspired us. I'll say that. We keep our garbage aboard until we get to port. We steer clear of whales. We don't let our men go out and buy shoes made of crocodile skin. You turned us around, Barry. Made us believers."

"I'm honored to hear you say that, captain. You're very kind. I hope that covers ancient Egyptian artifacts, as well."

The captain's aide, Lieutenant Morris Applegate, golden haired, blue eyed, young, seemed a bit edgy. "What you asked in your phone call to us is a little irregular," he said. "We have little experience in securing Egyptian tombs."

I knew they would have doubts, and I didn't much blame them. I smiled. "One chopper? Two men? One day? Two at the most. I didn't calculate that it would be a serious drain on your resources. Think of it as a training exercise, maybe?"

"With a pilot?"

"Of course. He'll come back after dropping your men."

"Where?"

"West of Saqqara. A canyon in the Wadi Faed."

"Not much out there."

I grinned. "Right now, there's a helluva lot out there."

"The Egyptians have hardware. We've trained them. You've inquired?"

"Yes, I'm aware of how competent they are. They have their hands full. Right now, there's no one in antiquities to confirm the orders. Any business regarding tombs is very sensitive in this country. One authority is down south. The other is in Greece. They'll handle this when they get back. I estimate a couple of days. I see it as a chance for a little American involvement. It would show American determination to help save heritage sites. The help to our cause would be far-reaching, I assure you."

Kane said: "They must not consider this matter an emergency."

I looked squarely at him. "I do. The fact is that the Egyptians have many emergencies. We are able to help...and I think we should."

The captain said: "You are very persuasive, Barry. I cannot fault your argument."

Applegate had a worried look. "You mentioned on the phone something about a threat to blow us up?"

"You. Some other vessel of the group. I don't have information yet on a specific target. You just happen to be the nearest."

The young lieutenant rolled his eyes. "We are constantly under threat. Someone always wants to blow us out of the water."

Kane asked: "Egyptian intelligence in on this?"

"I'm working with security. They have little to go on. On the other hand, they do know that the Black Robes want to render American installations uninhabitable."

"Nerve gas? Radiation?"

"Those are good enough guesses. Explosives is what I have now, though I don't know what kind. My line on this is a syndicate selling objects that they hope to get from the tombs in the Wadi Faed. Millions of dollars worth to support this effort."

"When will they make the sale?"

"Never, if I can help it. That's why I'm here. The tombs are unguarded at the moment."

The captain looked at the lieutenant. "Then we have time..."

The lieutenant looked at me. I said: "I'm not assuming so. My informant tells me that they have credit. The explosives are already purchased and loaded. We're running out of time. Pretty fast."

The captain asked: "What's your focus?"

"I'm trying to stop them from disturbing the artifacts. They went out last night to retrieve artifacts but we took their chopper away from them and I flew it back to Cairo."

The lieutenant was overwhelmed. "Jee-suss! Who's we?"

"I have two assistants. These thugs were about to go in and plunder. Screw up all the stuff before archeologists could get in and catalog the objects."

"Sounds like an interesting academic exercise."

That touched me with a flash of anger, but I didn't let it show. "I call it rape. Egypt has been ripped off for more than two thousand years and there's not much left. These tombs hold priceless objects that will open up one helluva lot of data on life in the time of the first Tuthmosis. If those bastards pull it out of there, we've lost all reference to relative locations of objects and burials in the tombs. That is critical mass in this business."

The lieutenant tried to be polite. "It isn't exactly our business."

I answered back immediately. "We're part of UNESCO. This is everybody's business. The U.S. is committed to help. Especially in an emergency. You've got thousands of guns fighting for your mission. We who are trying to save the world's heritage aren't quite as well equipped. Which is understating the matter. That's why I'm here."

Applegate said: "This felucca. The explosives. Do they think they can get close to us without interdiction?"

I shrugged my shoulders. "They must think it's worth a try. They must hope that you'll think they're a fishing boat. After all, you're in Egyptian waters."

The captain spoke now with a trace of impatience. "I think you can understand, Barry, despite all you've said, and I agree with it, that our basic responsibilities do not lie with the preservation of Egyptian antiquities."

Applegate, trying to make a few points in front of the boss, added: "Our mission in the Middle East is to secure the peace and prevent—."

This conversation was going into reverse. I pointed out that there wouldn't be much peace if these artifacts were sold and the proceeds used to disable the ship and its crew. Besides, time was of the essence. The robbers would head for the tombs again at any time.

The captain lapsed into thought for a moment. "I admit that we are permitting limited shore leave at the moment. But you understand that this region is continuously volatile."

"Granted, sir."

"We have a very limited supply of aircraft to devote to random purposes. We cannot be diverted in case of an alert. With available hardware restricted, I'm sorry to say..."

He was polite and beginning to get a little negative. I could not deny that in his position, utmost care is always exercised. I had hoped he would not start down this track, and I was ready for it. "I guess I was just thinking about the resources you do have out here," I said, "and I'm impressed. Besides your own group, you have six tactical units in the eastern Mediterranean under Colonel Jakes, two in Athens under General Brophy, and seven in Italy under Admiral Boatright. With supplies due tomorrow on the *Esmeralda*. Langdon has a British destroyer in Malta, and La Pierre a D'Estienne D'Orves frigate in Marseilles... Do you know La Pierre? Wonderful chap. I met him some time ago at the Sorbonne, where I was giving a lecture on international environmental law. March, a year ago, I think it was..."

I stopped. The captain smiled. The effect upon the lieutenant was immediate and stunning. His eyes flew wide open. He looked at me directly and intently. When he spoke, it was in hushed tones. "Jee-suss Ke-RIST, man. What is your security clearance? Where did you—?"

The captain said: "I wouldn't trifle with Dr. Ross, Morris. I don't know of any outsider as well connected as this guy. I'm not surprised. His level of information is not to be dismissed..."

"Gentlemen," I went on, "I have conferred with Egyptian military and security. I would not have made this request if it wasn't an emergency. The Egyptians are aware of why I am in Egypt. I am here by order of the United Nations. They are all informed of what I am trying to do. My office is in touch with Admiral Henry's staff in Washington. I'm confident they would approve of your dispatching a couple of men on, shall we say, a small mission of an unusual nature. I'm to keep the admiral posted."

I had never seen anyone as surprised as the Lieutenant. I had not intended to go this far, but neither did I have time to dally around.

Applegate was speechless. The captain smiled. "Oh, Barry, I can't help but be on your side in this, all else permitting. I suppose we should feel honored. We've never been asked to do quite this sort of thing before. I appreciate your devotion to saving the world heritage. We will be of service. With one proviso, I should add. In case something comes up—."

I held up my hand. "Captain, if you need to call your men back, without notifying me, I understand. That is your responsibility. I will appreciate any help you can provide."

The captain nodded, then addressed Applegate. "Is Thurston available?"

"Yes, sir."

"I think he's just the man."

Applegate left as the Swains swept in. After introductions, Veronica said: "Oh, Captain, we're just overwhelmed. Barry, this place is simply fantastic! It's a whole city. My god, it's... Do you know how many thousand people are on board?"

Tab said: "She gets very excited over these things."

"So do I," I responded.

I shook hands with the captain, excused us, and hustled the Swains out of there before they could let fly at each other.

THIRTY ONE

We flew back to the mainland with Lieutenant Thurston and two armed men.

It was late afternoon by the time we reconnoitered the junction of the Wadi Faed and Wadi Sostris, saw nobody, and settled down in front of the tombs. I took the men to the entrance, showed them where to place themselves and gave them instructions about what to do if anyone attempted to enter those caves. And if they got outnumbered, how to call for help.

"If you have to kill, kill," I said. "But try not to. The Egyptian government is behind us every step of the way."

They nodded and took up positions. I reboarded the chopper and we headed back to Cairo, the Swains protesting all the way about not being able to get "just one tiny peek inside the tombs."

"You'll get all the look you want," I promised, "if we can keep the thugs out of them. I'll give you a guided tour."

Lieutenant Thurston left us at the airport and flew back to the Atlantis. I dropped the Swains off at the hotel, with instructions to get in touch with Turki's replacement as soon as possible and get some Egyptian protection out to those tombs. "It will take time," I said, "because you may have to go through the bureaucracy."

"Do we have time?" Tab asked.

"No," I answered. "But get started on it anyway. It's all we can do."

"Where are you going?"

"I'm going to find out about that felucca."

Veronica looked worried. "You'll let us know?"

"Of course," I answered. "Keep your phone handy."

Within ten minutes, I was down on the dock, approaching the little shack. Zebec had taken Julie and Joe. It was time for a showdown.

Nobody around. I tried to go inside. The door was locked. I looked along the dock, hoping for sight of Apis. No sign of him, either.

I began to inquire, simply by asking: "Zebec?"

Five times I did this with passersby, and finally got an answer.

Zebec dead.

No reason. No explanation. Nothing.

Or else, no one on the docks of Cairo would talk. Not even for money. That I found hard to understand.

I stopped in my tracks. I had no reason to doubt it. I also had no reason to believe it, either. I didn't believe anything any more. Just the same, if it were true, then I had lost contact with the only person Apis had said could identify the mysterious Isis, mastermind of the syndicate. Whoever commanded this outfit could melt into the woodwork and rise up some other place to start another syndicate. Another shadowy effort to rob the world of its history.

Worse yet, I had lost connections with Julie and Joe.

Abject failure struck me on the head like the back end of a scimitar. Zebec was a man who killed others. Why and how could this happen? Dissension from within? Other syndicates? Enemies? Revenge? Little Apis had a scar on his forehead, courtesy of Zebec.

I started asking around for Apis.

No answers. Shrugs only.

It was getting dark. I was dead tired. The only place I wanted to go now was back to the hotel and get some sleep. Everything else had collapsed. I might as well, too. Maybe Apis would try to find me.

No point in waiting for a miracle, though. Not in Cairo. Not anywhere. I was in charge, and everything in sight had gotten screwed up.

Well, I didn't exactly beat my breast on the way back. I had been in such predicaments before. Plunged into the depths of despair...with no way out.

Everything was about to happen. Along this river was a felucca loaded with some kind of explosive. It might even now be on its way to the Mediterranean. Two men guarded the tombs, but they could be recalled at any moment. Maybelle's mob was out there trying to do something about Turki's death. And now, no Julie or Joe.

If this wasn't a fragile mess, I'd never seen one. Call it a house of glass, a house of cards. It was practically falling down already.

I tried not to ponder any more of this as I went up to the room, opened the door with care, checked the location of the shaving brush, the newspaper and the file folder, cleaned up, and fell in bed.

If there had been a cobra there, I wouldn't have known it.

THIRTY TWO

I waked glum and discouraged.

Della didn't help when she called to say that the carrier captain was going to have to call his men back from the tombs. Something about destabilization of the military situation.

"When?" I asked.

"Some time today."

"That's not much help."

"And Sam called to say that—."

"Fuck Sam!"

"You want me to tell him that?"

"I'm sorry, Della. This is not one of my better mornings. What did he have to say?"

"It was about Venezuela. I told him you'd decided on Australia and that I'd already gotten your tickets. He wasn't happy but he gave in. What's the matter in Cairo?"

"They've got Julie and Joe. The only guy who could tell me who Isis is was killed last night..."

"Who's Isis?"

"That's what I'd like to know. Head of the syndicate. I got the tombs covered, and now they're recalling the guards. There's a felucca loaded with tons of explosive heading for a carrier group in the Mediterranean."

"You want me to inform Admiral Henry's staff?"

"No. I don't have enough proof of anything to—. Oh, the hell with it. Anything else?"

"No. How've you been, Barry?"

"Fine. You, Della?"

"Great. 'Sta luego."

I called the Swains. If anybody could cheer me up, they could. They had changed their glowing scarlet caftans for practical field clothes, khaki shirts and trousers, with battered hats. That was to show that they meant business.

We breakfasted on rice and eggs at a little restaurant not far from Ezbekiya Gardens. I wasn't hungry because I was mad. Furious that everything was falling apart. I ate like a horse anyway...and listened.

"No contact with the antiquities office," Tab began. "Then we went back looking for that felucca. I think we examined every felucca from Saqqara to Heliopolis. No dice. How can we tell what's in all that cargo on any of them?"

"I could," Veronica said, admonishing him. "You just have to look close."

"Okay," he answered. "If you're so goddam smart, which one was it?"

I held up a hand. "Keep trying. I'm going to find Apis. He ought to know. Have you seen him lately?"

Tab: "No."

Veronica: "Yes."

I raised my eyebrows. "Where?"

"Once on the docks."

"When?"

"Yesterday. It was just a fleeting glimpse."

Tab frowned. "Ah, you were probably just seeing things. As usual."

"I was not. You were driving."

I asked: "What else? Any reports from the other guys?"

Veronica answered: "Nothing on syndicates. They don't get in the papers much."

"Isis?"

"Molly and Mei Hua have drawn a complete blank."

"Sandy take his equipment to the tombs?"

"He's ready, but he's concerned about the guards. If there's any trouble, he doesn't want his equipment damaged or stolen."

I frowned. We couldn't blame him. "The captain sent word that the Navy guards are to be withdrawn today. Can't the Egyptians get some guards out there?"

"Ali thinks they can. He's working on it. The new antiquities guy is due back from Greece this morning."

This was much too slow a process. "Can you get Sandy to help on that, reinforce Ali?"

"Sure. He wants to. No promises, though."

"Let me know instantly, either way."

"Roger."

THIRTY THREE

Trying once again to reach Julie and Joe at Club Med, I got nothing.

This now sent a red alert through my brain. If they were in trouble—and I could only assume so—then I had to drop everything and find them.

Exasperated, I had only one avenue of search: Apis. With Zebec dead, my negotiations with the syndicate were lost. Joe's and Julie's negotiations must also be at a standstill. Or worse. If the syndicate were really coming apart, Apis, too, may have paid a price. Maybe Apis and Zebec had fought a pitched battle. I doubted if the police would know anything of it. Nothing that deep down in the black hole...

If Apis had been wiped out, too, that would be a disastrous setback. He had information I needed. Maybe he could tell me about Julie and Joe. And if he didn't know who Isis was, at least he knew Isis existed.

He also knew about the deadly felucca, which might at this moment be on its way down the Nile, headed for the carrier.

On the way to the docks, I called Della and instructed her to have the Navy send a helicopter to pick me up at the airport in two hours. She didn't know whether she could, and neither did I.

"Tell them," I suggested to her, "that I need reconnaissance. I want to hunt down that felucca I told the carrier captain about."

"Where are you going now?" she asked. "Will I be able to reach you?"

"Yes. I'll be down along the docks. I've got to find Julie and Joe, and the only human being who can tell me where they are is Apis, the little guy from the syndicate. If he's still alive."

"Good luck."

"Thanks, Della."

Down on the docks, I found lots of people and lots of activity, but no one I knew. I tried the little shack. People in there I didn't recognize. I decided not to ask around for Apis. It was just a hunch, but with things so destabilized, it seemed better to poke around on my own, without help. If that didn't work, I would try hiring someone to lead me to the little guy.

Sauntering along like a tourist, acting nonchalant, I nevertheless let my eyes dart into every corner, every open door, every houseboat, every barge being loaded, every dhow, felucca, motorboat with the commerce of Cairo. In places there were boats hooked to boats by chain and rope. How I wished for a dog that could sniff explosives—which, of course, would make me about as obvious as the pyramids.

There was every kind of parcel and container, covered by every kind of tarp, net, and canvas, or stowed in nylon bags—if the cargo were covered at all. In this climate, shippers worried little about rain. Dust was far more prevalent. The feluccas were loaded with boxes, foodstuffs, ropes, poles, carpets, oil, old battered irrigation pumps, baskets, backpacks, and sacks of who-knows-what.

I was in over my head, and I knew it, but swimming for life...

Restaurants sat at the water's edge, as though ready to float away, and I walked along the verandas of these, peering inside as though looking for a friend, or a husband searching for a wife, trying to glimpse any familiar face.

It was useless, as I knew it would be, trying to find one person in a city of twenty million. I sauntered back. If Apis had been able to glimpse me, perhaps he would come forward. A remote and desperate hope at best. I kidded myself that maybe he had been looking for me ever since our meeting. That he had something else to tell me. Or sell me. That he was on my side.

If this went on much longer, they could cart me away in a strait-jacket. I had no other direct sources of information about the syndicate. I had interviewed Maybelle's mob, at least the ones I had met that first night. Except for Molly Holly. Only the Swains had been of direct help, pushing me toward Apis.

In my mind, I went over again and again that conversation with the little bull. I had asked him when the felucca would sail. He had said he knew nothing. He only pointed to the sun and walked away.

What did that mean? Could it have been that by the time the sun came around again to the same place in the sky, the explosives would be floating down the Nile? I seemed to be drifting without any answers, like the waters of the Nile drifting from the mountains of Ethiopia down to the delta, shifting, flowing, eddying, whirling... I had been caught in a backwater of Cairo, looking for an obscure, nonexistent...

In this reverie, I came back to the little shack and sat for a while on a box. The air had a dream-like texture, blurring the boats and buildings, muffling the million voices that seemed to drift across the city and across the Nile. The brown sky blended with a thousand faces that merged before me into one, the little man with the scar on his—.

He put his hand on my shoulder, uncertain whether I was dozing or in deep meditation.

I shook my head, clearing the liquid air, sharpening the focus of minarets in the distance, and looked into the eyes of the little man with the scar on his forehead.

 THIRTY FOUR

Trying not to look completely stunned with surprise, I let my eyes fall.

Apis sat in front of me.

I pulled out a hundred-dollar bill and let it drift to the ground before him. To my astonishment, he picked it up and handed it back to me.

It took a few moments to decipher that one. I could only conclude that he wanted to help me now, not for himself but for the sake of Egypt. Many times I had relied upon this before, from the Amazon to the islands of the Pacific, upon the principle that patriotism means more to a great many people than nearly anything else. In many a little and lonely soul it builds up into a force more powerful than greed, transcending even survival itself.

I showed no surprise. I accepted it as normal, and put the money back in my pocket, not trying to force him to take it. My role now was to play his obedient servant. He had something to tell me, or he would not have come to me. I would not hurry it, much as I wanted like the devil to find out what was going on. To show him respect—which he apparently got little of in his lifetime—I said nothing. But by that token, I said that I was listening.

I dared not even move. I stifled my desire for him to start talking, lest he run away and disappear again among the twenty million faces of Cairo.

He did not talk. Instead, he pointed toward a felucca in the distance. After running one hand up in the air to signify the tall mast and sail of the river vessel, he spread his hands to form a big bulging parcel at the base of the mast. Cargo.

He closed his fists, then suddenly opened them in a sweep of arms that meant, I was sure, an explosion.

This is where we had ended our last conversation. The felucca laden with explosives.

Now he pointed down the Nile, holding his left hand steady and running his right hand straight down in the direction of the river flow. It could only mean that the felucca had sailed. I thrust my hands forward a couple of times to verify whether the boat had sailed. He nodded.

Apis was a master of expressive sign language. I found no difficulty in deciphering his arm and hand movements, even though his face remained a mask. He never once looked at me to see whether I understood. His motions, deliberate and slow, were meant to convey ideas clearly, and that they did.

Next, he pointed to me. Then he raised a hand with the fingers pointing to the sky. Immediately following that, he took the two index fingers and pointed them to the sky alongside where the hand that represented me had been.

Sidekicks! My exultation at these revealing signs—if, of course, I guessed correctly—knew no bounds. But I kept it all within, as though I expected him to disappear in a flash and the image lost. I nodded that I understood.

His hands then formed an oval-shaped package, a repetition of the cargo of the felucca...the explosives on board. Pointing his two index fingers in the sky, to indicate my sidekicks, he then curved one of the fingers and pointed directly to the explosives.

I shuddered. If that meant what I thought it did, then Julie and Joe were *on top of the explosive cargo.*

Apis crossed his wrists and rubbed them together, then crossed them again behind his back. That said to me that Julie and Joe were prisoners, their hands tied behind their backs. He formed the oval bulk of the cargo again, and pushed both hands forcibly down toward it.

They were strapped to the cargo.

He then slowly twisted his hands into a palms up position, meaning that that was as far as he could go, that he had no more information, and that all was lost with Julie and Joe.

They had been hijacked. Taken hostage. My shock at this revelation was tempered by the fact that it was actually quite a brilliant move on the part of the syndicate. It assured them, as far as their twisted minds could see, safe passage to the carrier. Within range, they would detonate the cargo, taking themselves and Julie and Joe to the next world. Along with hundreds of sailors and jet aircraft.

I could not conceive that such a bold plan could be even proposed, much less devised in such a complex way. No one could get near one of those carriers without interdiction. They would be blown out of the water while yet miles away.

I didn't kid myself. Sometimes crazy things succeed in this part of the world. It wasn't the first time that terrorists had proposed to blow up American military installations, and some of the others had triumphed with all too grisly results. No matter how daring, even the faintest hint of success could be all the terrorists needed. If the little ship with the tall sail looked innocent enough—and Egypt had lots of feluccas—perhaps they could get away with it. Don't merchants come to ships to sell trinkets?

They could not possibly have determined how much a hole their cargo might blow in the side of the carrier. It had never been done before. There were no measurements. But if a truck bomb could destroy a twelve story building, a felucca with a larger cargo could make quite a hole. The advantage to their brains must have been that a good-sized hole could sink the ship.

Martyr heaven would have no braver souls.

These thoughts whirled through my mind with the passage of only a few seconds. And in the next few seconds, I knew exactly what I had to do.

THIRTY FIVE

Without another moment's hesitation, I grasped Apis's arm as gently as I could, paused only long enough to ask him silently if he would come with me. He offered no resistance.

With that, we dashed up to my car and got inside.

On the way to the airport, I called Della. The Navy, she reported, couldn't get a helicopter to me before 1800 hours. Something about the military situation. They tried their best, she said, but couldn't. I said okay, to forget it. I would try to get a machine at the airport, rent one if I had to.

Meanwhile, would she issue a stop-payment order on the check that the Mucks must have written for the artifacts they didn't get?

"What did you say?" she asked.

"Julie and Joe must have been forced to sign over a check to these guys. I don't know for sure, of course, but it's a precaution. Call Kelly's bank and make sure payment is stopped."

"Can I do that? It's not my bank."

"You'd better."

"Thanks."

"If you get any flak, call Kelly. I don't know how much the check was written for, but it was our plan to stop payment anyway."

"Okay. Brasher called from Cairns."

"I'll be there as soon as I can."

"That's what I told him. Sam also called..."

"About Venezuela?"

"Yes."

"How you been, Della?"

"Fine, Barry. You?"

"Great. Zai jian, zai jian."

"Zai jian."

I contacted the Swains and told them to stand by, that the felucca had sailed, it was on its way down the Nile, and I had Apis in tow. We were going to try to find the vessel from the air. They said they were ready to set off at once down the main highway, keeping the river in sight. But someone had to tell them which branch of the Nile and which boat was which.

By the time we got to the airport, it was almost noon. I took Apis to lunch and while waiting ran into my first piece of good luck in days.

I had left the table briefly to see if I could rent a helicopter. Outside I ran into Amir, the pilot who had taken us out to the tombs. With him was Dr. Gholub, Turki Husseini's replacement in the department of antiquities. He was bulky, bespectacled, wore a white hat and seersucker suit, and shook my hand with such vigor that I almost lost three fingers.

"Dr. Ross! How lucky my day this is! Everybody tells me about you, and when I think I meet you, then I go to Greece. Oh, this is terrible. You are working on Turki's death. Poor Turki. What you learn? Anything?"

"Not much," I responded, with a note of despair in my voice for effect. "My concern is for the tombs out there in the Wadi Faed..."

"I am just going out there with Mr. Santano."

"Is Sandy here?"

"Not yet. We expect him in minutes."

"Wait. Why don't you come and have lunch with us? Both of you?"

Amir nodded. When we got to the table, I introduced Apis to them. Gholub talked with the little bull in Arabic for a while, then said: "Praise be to Allah. Dr. Ross, you have somehow got a right man. He knows everything going on."

"Well, not everything," I corrected. "But he's a great help. Can you ask him if he would know that felucca if he saw it?"

Gholub spread his hands and rolled his eyes in the sky. "Oh, well, there are so many feluccas in Egypt. Most of them look alike. I think you must be making joke."

"Can you ask him?"

More conversation in Arabic. Apis shrugged his shoulders.

Gholub replied: "He's not sure."

Then I tried another long shot. "Would you ask him who Isis is?"

"I can answer that. Wife of Osiris, Mother of Horus..."

"No, no. Isis is the code name for the head of the syndicate that is robbing tombs and taking the artifacts out. I must find out who this is."

A clipped conversation in Arabic, ending quickly.

Gholub to me: "He doesn't have the slightest idea. I think he's honest about that."

I changed the subject, told Gholub all I knew about the tombs and the syndicate, and that I didn't think that any more of the artifacts had been taken away.

"You're going out there right now?"

"Soon, yes."

"Are you taking guards with you?"

Gholub nodded. "Two military men."

"Good. I was about to find a helicopter to take Apis and me to the carrier."

Gholub spread his arms again, like the wings of an ancient bird, and became animated with that famous Egyptian hospitality that I had known so well. "Oh! Let me help. Amir can take you. Right now. We are only waiting for Mr. Santano."

It was exactly what I had hoped he would say, but I warned him that it might take an hour or two. "I want Apis to identify the felucca."

Gholub guffawed, and slapped me on the shoulder. "What is time? In Egypt? Dr. Ross, we have more time than anything. It is free."

I grabbed his hand and thanked him. While we ate, I called the Swains and told them to get on the road and head down the delta.

"Which road?" Veronica asked. "Which branch of the Nile? Do you know that yet?"

"I would guess that they will take the west branch toward Rosetta. Get on the road that goes along the edge of the valley toward El Khatatba."

"Where?"

"Near the ruins of Kom Abu Billo."

"Gotcha."

"We'll be overhead as soon as we can get there."

THIRTY SIX

After lunch, Amir led Apis and me to the far side of the landing field, where we boarded the same Bell Long Ranger that I had flown back from the Wadi Faed. The Egyptian government had confiscated it.

The eyes of the little bull were wide with excitement. For all I knew, it was his first time in a helicopter, first time in the air. I had asked Dr. Gholub to brief Apis on where we were going and that all we wanted him to do was identify the felucca, if he could.

Sitting at the window, the little bull became agitated with excitement as we rose above Cairo and headed down the Nile.

Once again, I was struck with the utter contrast of the rich, irrigated greenery of the delta—tomato fields and cotton plantations—and the brooding, merciless desert, hot as blazes and dry as bone.

White-sailed feluccas everywhere! That was the problem. I despaired that Apis could pick out one among the many.

We picked up the Swains about thirty miles down the Nile, past the point where the great river divides into its two main channels. We flew high, and I could see them in their Land Rover, waving to us.

"Barry, is that you?" Veronica shouted into her phone.

"Yes," I replied. "Stand by with an open mike. If we're on the right track we should have a visual sighting any time."

"Roger."

I looked at Apis. Nothing yet.

I'd given instructions to Amir not to fly too low. I no way wanted to alert the boatmen on the deadly felucca that they were being followed.

Just beyond Khatatba, where the Nile makes a big loop toward the west and back, Apis became very excited, pulled my elbow and pointed downward.

I immediately said to Veronica: "Stand by. I think Apis has something."

I leaned over. The numbers of vessels on the water had diminished, and Apis was able to point out one that had navigated the loop and was heading north.

Staring at Apis, I made a face that meant: "Are you sure?"

He nodded vigorously.

"Okay, Veronica, he seems to be sure of it. You're not there yet, but the Nile loops to the west, and the felucca has just gone around the loop."

"Okay, Barry. Anything special about it?"

"Not that I can see from up here."

"It was a silly question."

"There's some kind of an awning to keep the sun out. I can barely see some blue and white stripes. I can't see into the boat and tell whether Julie and Joe are aboard. That's for you to determine."

"We'll do it."

"Be careful," I warned. "I don't want those guys to think they're being chased. If you stop just opposite them, or go back and forth, or get out and watch them with binoculars while they pass, they'll get nervous."

"Understood, Barry. We'll reduce our speed a little, but we'll go right on by."

"After you get downstream out of sight, maybe you can hide your car and get out and observe them from behind some grass or something."

"Good idea."

"Get a fix on that felucca. Try to see if Julie and Joe are tied up."

"You're kidding."

"No. Just grasping at straws."

"How can we be sure this is the boat?"

I smiled. "If you could see Apis right now, you'd know."

"We'll take his word for it."

"We are going to fly on down the river and out to the carrier. As soon as you come into eye contact, let me know at once. Keep your channel open."

Not for fifteen minutes was there any response. I asked Amir to circle inland for a little while, out of sight of the river. I would feel better about going to the carrier if I could get some kind of ground-level fix on that boat.

"We see it!" Veronica shouted. "Barry, are you there?"

"I'm here. What does it look like?"

"Barry, I'm sorry to have to tell you, it looks like any other felucca. Pretty big one, though. We can see blue and white stripes on the awning."

"Sitting low in the water?"

"How do I know?"

"Never mind. Any flags of any kind?"

"Nothing. I don't think they want to be conspicuous. But I did put my binoculars on it, and I saw a male and female silhouetted aboard. They looked like tourists."

"How many boatmen?"

"Two is all we saw. May be others sleeping and out of sight."

"Anything else?"

"We've gone beyond them now. But we'll try to hole up somewhere and hide the Land Rover and get a good look as they go by."

"Good going! Hang in there, Veronica. We're going on out to the carrier. The felucca is not going to make it before nightfall, so you'll have to hole up somewhere."

"No problem for us."

"You can power off, now. But call me the first chance you get."

"We will. We're in charge here!"

That sounded ominous, but I tried not to pay any attention to it.

THIRTY-SEVEN

Amir settled onto the carrier deck, let us out, and flew back to the mainland.

Apis was more wide-eyed than ever. I thought he was going to twist his neck out of shape gawking at all the aircraft aboard. There was little action just now, but he had never been on a landing field at sea, and that was excitement enough for him. The sheer immensity of the vessel, 1,000 feet long and 24 stories high, was impressive by any standard.

I had to take some pains to explain to the Captain and Lieutenant that Apis was a collaborator on our side, and had been instrumental in identifying the felucca that was at this moment sailing down the Nile toward the Atlantis.

Applegate seemed genuinely surprised. "How did you get his collaboration?"

I pointed to the scar on the little guy's face. "See that? It was administered by his boss with a rawhide quirt. These syndicates play rough."

"Defector?"

"Yes. Without him we couldn't have done it. He spotted the felucca just this side of El Khatatba."

"Hundred per cent sure it was the right felucca?"

"Apis was. And we have a team—you met the Swains—in a Land Rover on the road, tracking them. What we don't know is how long it will take the felucca to get here."

The lieutenant got out a map and made some brief calculations. "Feluccas move slowly…"

"Unless they have a motor."

"Did you see evidence of that?"

"No."

"Have you informed Egyptian security?"

At this question, the captain looked at me intently, and I wasn't sure why. Probably he knew a lot more about Middle East terrorism than I did. Seeing his concern, I took care to explain my options carefully. "I am working with Security on the Turki Husseini murder. They have warned me, however, that they can't be of much help. They have their hands full with bombings of Coptic churches in the south, militant threats, and Allah knows what else."

"The military?"

"I have determined to keep the police and military in reserve. With Julie and Joe aboard, I don't want anyone getting close to that ship. It's bad enough as it is. There could be some accident even now that could blow them to kingdom come."

The captain seemed relieved. "I agree with you there. We have the means to handle this ourselves."

That statement sent a chill down my spine, and he saw the worried look on my face. He clarified his meaning. "I'm sorry, Barry, that they are using your two assistants as shields, as hostages. I don't see any place here for negotiation."

"Meaning?"

"If what you say is true, and we are their intended target, we will not allow them to get close."

"Then what?" I asked the question although I knew the answer.

"We have various ways of taking them out of the water."

I paused for a moment and shifted my eyes from the captain to the lieutenant and back. "You'd blow them up."

"They should be aware that if they get too close, they will be stopped. We'll warn them, of course, send out a helo. My guess is that they want to be blown up and they will try to get as close as possible to this ship before they provoke us into it."

I paused and looked up at the ceiling for a moment. "Tell me, Captain, how close is too close?"

He countered with a question of his own. "How much explosive is aboard? And what type?"

"I have no idea. My assumption is that they are sophisticated enough to get the biggest bang for their buck. If what they have is ammonium nitrate, then the stuff is pretty stable. But, as you know, it is difficult to detonate. They would have to have some kind of primer that would set off a booster, like T.N.T., to get enough of a shock wave to detonate the ammonium nitrate."

The captain nodded. "I would not put it beyond their capability. Can you estimate how much is aboard?"

I pointed to Apis. "All I can get from this little guy is that the felucca—" here I swung my arms in a wide sweep "—will go BOOM! That help any?"

The captain smiled. "Yes. I think that's all we need to know. I will set a limit of three kilometers. If they come inside that range, we will disable them."

It was a polite term, but I knew what he meant.

"Now," I said, "what are your options? Anything besides blowing it up?"

"I can't think of any."

"What about backing up?"

The captain frowned. "Barry, I think you can understand the strategy of containment."

I did, but I didn't like it. I stalled for time. "Containment?"

"When you get a floating time bomb out on the Mediterranean, your first priority is to remove it. There are other ships and subs out here and we don't want this felucca running into any of them."

There was no denying the captain's rationale. All I could see was Julie and Joe tied up and waiting to be incinerated in the explosion.

"We do have one other possibility," Applegate said. "We could attempt an interdiction from below. From underneath the surface."

I had been mulling that over for some time, and told him so. "To approach the boat in daylight, your men would leave a trail of bubbles. The trigger-happy terrorists would see that. To approach from beneath would require your men to come out of the water and peek over the gunwale. I just don't believe that anyone on earth could move fast enough to leap on deck and get to those guys before they let loose with their automatic rifles. If you tried to fire at them, they could drop, and you'd have a firefight on your hands in the utmost of sensitive places. With Julie and Joe right in the middle. We have a hazardous situation driven by religion, by fanaticism, in which there are no rules. You kill or get killed."

Captain: "To this I must agree. I know we could find volunteers, but at this point I don't think I could bring myself to consider that option."

"So, then," I mused, "I have to find some other options…"

The lieutenant asked, bluntly: "What are they, sir? You can't get close to the felucca. You can't fire on it, for fear of setting everything off. You can't negotiate. You can't turn this whole thing over to the Egyptians and walk away from it. The guys on that felucca are stubborn as hell, and no one's going to talk them out of it. It looks to me like we're stuck with it. I've been trying to figure this out, sir, because I know how you feel. But to me it looks like a no win situation from every angle. You might as well—and I'm sorry to have to say this—stick around and watch the fireworks."

THIRTY EIGHT

The lieutenant took Apis and me below to a vacant officer's quarters with two bunks. There, we would sleep the night. I expected it to be a long night, waiting for what I felt was going to be a fateful and disastrous morning. He invited us to dine that evening in the officer's mess, and left.

The little bull curled up on one of the bunks for a nap. Climbing up on deck, I called Della. Nothing new there. I tried to reach Dr. Gholub's office, with no success. I could only assume that the guards and Sandy Santano had been taken to the tombs. No matter. There was nothing I could do about it anyway.

I tried to call Hami. No luck. Ali Fawzi. No luck. Ditto Molly Holly. Ditto Mei Hua. Where *was* everybody?

It was going on sunset by the time I reached the Swains. They reported that they had had a devil of a time tracking the felucca and staying out of sight. They had become lost on side roads trying to backtrack, gotten mired in mud trying to cross an irrigated field and return to the main route.

"Where's the felucca now?"

Veronica's voice sounded tired. "I'll be damned if I know."

"You've lost it?"

"No, it's just that they've stopped beside somebody's rice field. We're nowhere. We're going to sleep beside the Land Rover about a mile away."

"Can you tell how far you are from the coast?"

"On the map it looks like maybe twenty kilometers."

From this I concluded that the boatmen were going to stay for the night and not come on out into the open sea after dark. "Have you heard whether Gholub and Santano got out to the tombs?"

"Not a word."

"What's the holdup?"

"Unknown."

"Then there was no one there last night?"

"Apparently not. Not that we've heard."

"What about Hami, Ali, Molly and Mei Hua? I've been trying to get in touch with them."

"Oh, they're on their way to Alexandria."

She said it in such a matter-of-fact way that I thought I had misunderstood.

"What did you say?"

"They're on their way to Alexandria."

I still didn't believe my ears. And I didn't think I was going to like what I heard. "What on earth for?"

The hair was beginning to stand up on the back of my neck. I had a way of smelling disaster from a mile away.

Veronica sounded rather proud of herself. "Well, we kind of got together, phonewise, and they think it just ain't right for you to have to shoulder all this responsibility by yourself while they remain in Cairo."

I said quickly: "That's my job. I'm trained for it. I'm paid for it. I'm used to it. Don't tell me—."

"Well, Ali took the lead. He's the only Egyptian among us, and he speaks Arabic and he thought it would be a good idea if maybe we tried to talk these guys out of what we think they're going to do."

My throat tightened so much that for a moment I couldn't answer. All I needed was for a bunch of amateurs to start gumming up the works. Not that anything was laid out beautifully for a rescue. But amateurs stumbling into a situation like this could only make it worse...get themselves and others killed.

"Barry? You still there?"

"I'm still here, Veronica. Aren't you the slightest bit aware of how dangerous that would be?"

"Of course, I am. You don't know what I talked them out of."

"You talked them out of something?"

She giggled. "Yes. As soon as I told them where we were and what we were doing, they hatched up a scheme to sneak up on the felucca and shoot the boatmen."

"You're kidding?"

"Certainly not. They thought it would be neat and surgical, and would be over in less than a minute."

"They didn't think that any gunplay could set off the explosives? Or that Julie and Joe would get shot?"

"That's what I told them. Believe me, Barry, it took me ten minutes to talk them out of that. They are so mad at those guys, and so grateful to you, they are determined to do something."

"Uh, what kind of something did they decide on?"

This conversation seemed like it was coming from another world. I didn't have a solution myself to this problem, but neither did they. Not an intelligent one, anyway. I'd had commando training. I knew how to sneak up on redoubts and capture the enemy. Pursuit and arrest call for specialized skills. I had them. They didn't. But sneak up on the felucca, startle the gunmen, engage in a pitched battle?

Goodbye, Julie and Joe.

Veronica went on. "They compromised. They will rent a speedboat in Alexandria and go along the coast until they see the felucca. Then they will go on board and talk the guys out of what they're doing."

This froze me with horror. All I could say, weakly, was: "Just like that?"

"Ali's pretty confident he can pull this off."

I barked sharply into the phone. "Well, godammit! I'm not!"

Veronica seemed surprised. "Barry! What's the matter?"

"I never heard of a lousier scheme to screw up the whole thing."

"Why? What do you mean?"

"Well, for one thing, they could all get nicely sprayed with automatic rifle fire as they approach."

"They are perfectly aware of that. They're not a bunch of nincompoops."

That gave me an opening, but I let it pass. "When they get within three kilometers of the carrier, the felucca will be blown out of the water and they will all go with it. Not to mention Julie and Joe. They are endangering the lives of everyone within a square mile."

"You said three kilometers?"

"From the carrier. Yes."

"I don't think they know that."

"Of course they don't! Do they expect the carrier captain to invite the felucca alongside?"

"Barry, I don't know what to think."

"I suppose you are going with them?"

"We're going to keep track of the felucca until it sails out into the Mediterranean."

I felt a little relief from that. "You, at least, have brains. Can you get in touch with any of them? They have to be stopped."

"Why? Give me just one good reason."

"They're archeologists, not diplomats."

"That doesn't matter to them. They perceive it as a mission. All they're trying to do is help you out. I think they're heroes."

"Veronica, heroism has nothing to do with this because it's all based on ignorance. You tell them that I don't *want* them to help me out. This is just too goddammed sensitive and dangerous. They'll get in the way."

"Of what? You have another plan? If you do you'd better let us know."

"I don't have another plan. Theirs is as harebrained as I've ever heard. Can you get in touch with them?"

"They don't have cell phones."

"Oh, shit!"

"What did you say?"

"Never mind. You don't know where they're spending the night in Alexandria?"

"No."

"That's what I mean. They go off on a wild chase without either contact or coordination."

"Well, I'll admit they were kinda swayed by Ali. He said he's an Egyptian. He knows Egyptians better than the rest of us. He knows how to talk them out of things like this."

My answer was as blunt as I could make it. "How the hell does he know the boatmen are Egyptians?"

Now there was a silence at Veronica's end of the line. "Oh, my god!"

"I thought so. You don't go into a project like this by the seat of your pants. I am deeply grateful for what they are trying to do to help. But I want them to drop their plans. Is there no way you can get word to them?"

"No."

"Go hunt for them?"

"You know how big Alexandria is?"

I sighed in desperation. "Then we're stuck with this?"

She let her words gush in a flood. "Barry, maybe they *can* do something. Maybe they *can* help. It could be that this harebrained scheme of theirs will work. Why not give them a chance?"

"Because there isn't a chance in hell that it could succeed."

"Don't you even give them credit for trying?"

"They will get themselves killed. And Julie and Joe in the bargain. I want them out of it. I don't want them anywhere near that felucca."

"Sorry, Barry. If that's the way you feel, I suppose they would hold back. But no guarantee, mind you. Now it's gone too far. If I were you, I'd just sit back and watch."

"That's what the lieutenant here said. Watch the fireworks."

THIRTY NINE

Tab came on the line. "Okay, Barry. If you think they are in such danger, we'll go rent a boat and go out and help them. Or turn them back."

I was aghast. "Tab, are you out of you mind?"

"It's logical. Look, we've been used to fighting each other for years."

"What is that supposed to mean?"

"We've been fighting Turki Husseini for years."

I was shaking my head. "Are you guys bent on suicide?"

"Come on. We know a little Arabic."

"Not enough for this. You're dealing with what we presume to be dedicated terrorists. Dedicated to blowing up that carrier, and neither you nor Ali, nor a thousand archeologists in all Egypt are going to stop them."

"Then we'll die trying."

"I don't want anyone to die. It's the silliest thing I've ever heard of. You guys won't stand a chance."

"This is our fight."

"It's mine, and I want you and Veronica and all of the rest of them to stay out of it. Stand by until tomorrow morning and I'll give you a call at sunup. You can tell us when the felucca heads out into the Mediterranean. After that, your job is done. Is that clear?"

No answer. I could hear him conferring with Veronica. I knew I had no authority to demand that they desist from anything. I knew they were stubborn, and when they got something in mind you could look for snowballs in hell before they turned back.

Tab came back on. "Where will you be, Barry?"

"What do you mean?"

"I mean tomorrow morning as the felucca approaches the ship."

"On board the carrier. Praying for Julie and Joe."

"Okay. Have no fear, Barry. You just leave this to us." With that, he powered off.

I put my phone back in my pocket and stood there stunned. I felt a rush to call the Alexandrian police and put a tail on Ali and company. That would be fruitless. I didn't know what kind of vehicle they were driving or what hotel they were in. If any. They could be staying with some of Ali's friends somewhere out along an irrigation canal.

I could send the police after the Swains...

In the end, I gave it up. There comes a time when you have to know when to quit, when the burden of events is so overwhelming that any procedure at all will be fruitless.

I was trapped. As trapped as if my leg had been caught in a bear trap.

Everything I didn't want to happen was all set to go. All arranged. All planned. And no way to stop it.

I felt worst about Julie and Joe. I couldn't call them. They sat there ready for the slaughter.

And yet, I had trained them on escape methods. It was the only option left. They were resourceful. They would get out of it by themselves.

I kidded myself for entertaining such a vain hope. There they were tied up and guarded. Guarded by fanatics who would shoot them at the slightest provocation.

The rest of the afternoon I walked around in a daze, staring out to sea, never wanting to see a felucca sail again. I scarcely heard any conversation at officer's mess. There wasn't much, anyway, because everyone else was as gloomy as I was.

I went to bed trying to think what I would tell Kelly, Sam, Joe's parents, Julie's parents, Maybelle. I would resign. UNESCO could get someone else to work on the spreading virus on Dinkum Island on the Great Barrier Reef. I would be disgraced. A hotshot like me is supposed to succeed, not fail. I could go somewhere and start up a little private practice, taking on divorce cases.

No one would want Barry Ross on any kind of assignment again.

My inner voice was merciless. *You sure as hell fucked it up this time, buddy. It's easy to say that someone else did it for you. You're not going to get away with that. Why didn't you reckon on those archeologists muscling in on this? Why didn't you keep closer track of Julie and Joe? It's all your fault, and come the devil in May, you're going to have to take all the blame...blame...blame...*

I tossed and turned, and finally fell asleep thinking of Julie and Joe. A young couple with promising careers. Deprived of their honeymoon. Two of the finest people I know. Two of the best helpers a person could ever have.

Going up in a ball of fire.

FORTY

I'll never forget the first time I met Joe. We were in a dugout canoe with a group of tourists in the Amazon basin of Colombia, heading down the Orteguasa River to stay with Correguaje Indians for a week.

Joe was a young biology graduate of the University of Wyoming, come to the Amazon to start work on a master's thesis. He was outspoken, irreverent, and brash. I like that in a person. When our canoe nudged up to the primitive dock where we would take the trail to the Correguaje village, he saw a log cabin perched on poles and hanging out over the water.

"What's that?" he asked.

I said "It's a place for the elimination of internal pressures."

"You mean a shit house?" he asked.

We had a rather distinguished group aboard—Oxford professors, computer engineers and the like—and I told him I was trying to find a term more suitable for a cultured society. Like "loo," perhaps.

"Where's the cultured society?" he asked.

Now I thought of that trip as I showered. Down here in the bowels of the carrier we could see no sunlight, didn't even know that the sun had risen. My watch told me it had, but I entertained no particular desire to go up on deck and see it. For as soon as the sun rose, so would the sail of the dread felucca, with Julie and Joe trapped aboard, sitting on tons of explosive.

Apis seemed cheerful enough, examining everything in sight. He reveled at eating in officer's mess, but my mind was a half a world away. Back in the Amazon forest...

The night we had arrived at the Correguaje village, the Indians hosted us at a feast where we sat on the ground and our food was served on fragments of palm leaves. Joe would look at his dish and, being ever curious and cautious, ask what it was.

Monty Adams, our guide, suggested that it would be better not to ask.

"I'll say," Joe responded. "This stuff is *moving!*"

They brought in another plate and ladled some odd-looking victual onto his palm leaf, and once again, irrepressibly curious, he asked what it was.

I responded: "Come on, Joe, I've eaten ash porridge and rotten fly soup with the Yanomamis of South America and grubs with the aborigines of Australia. You have to get used to this. You wanted adventure, didn't you? You said so."

I'll never forget his response as he paused, looked down at the piles of unidentifiable food before him, then up at me with a plaintive look on his face. "This is adventure?"

I grew to have great respect for the guy on that trip. When I had to enforce discipline among warring parties, he stood to back me up. We had one helluva murder on our hands, a thousand miles from nowhere, and his bravery and performance were tremendous. I thought that if I was going to clean up the world and save its wildlife, I could use someone like him. At the end of the trip, I hired him on the spot.

So deeply was I into these musings that I almost didn't hear Lieutenant Applegate's announcement: "Felucca approaching at 135 degrees."

The last thing I wanted to do was go up on the bridge. I steeled myself and finished breakfast. Apis did the same. I dawdled...delayed... Studied the picture of Admiral Henry on the wall... Mused over the map of the Mediterranean... My stomach tightened, arms became limp, eyes tried not to see, ears tried not to hear...

By the time Apis and I got to the bridge, I couldn't see the felucca anywhere. Without a word, the captain handed me a powerful pair of binoculars, and pointed to the southeast.

There it was, sure enough, just appearing on the horizon.

FORTY ONE

I turned to the captain and tried to raise a sickly smile.

"Good morning, captain," I said.

"Good morning, Barry. You slept well?"

"I always do. Today, getting up was the problem."

The captain looked out toward the horizon. When he spoke, it was with a genuinely sympathetic tone. "Believe me, Barry...I can understand."

"I dearly love those kids. They are hard workers, brave... God, do you know that I helped rescue Julie when she was clinging to a cliff in the Grand Canyon, dangling out over five thousand feet of open space? Someone had pushed her..."

"*Pushed* her?" The captain was incredulous.

"She was Inner Canyon Ranger last summer, and Joe and I were taking Hounto Chala, a high exec of the UN Environment Programme, down through the canyon on the Colorado River. Assassins were after him, and we had a murder, and a helluva time finding out who did it. Turned out to be the same person who pushed her off the edge."

The captain shook his head. "Jesus, you get into as much trouble as I do, Barry."

"Well, I guess now we're getting close to decision time."

The captain looked out the window. "I'm afraid we've reached it."

I followed his gaze, and the felucca's tall sail was just becoming visible to the naked eye.

"No other way?" I asked, forlornly.

He looked at me and then lowered his eyes. "I've got a billion-dollar ship here, with five thousand men aboard. If there were some other way, I'd use it."

He didn't have to say anything else. All I had was one little sailing vessel with two Americans aboard.

I understood all too well. I would have made the same decision if I had been wearing his braid. The felucca would have to be blown out of the water. I would have to witness it. Watch the two people I had brought over here get blown to pieces. The captain asked if there was any chance they could break free on their own.

"Of course," I replied. "They are trained in escape procedures. If they are tied to the deck, I would imagine that they have cut their ropes by now. They wear belts like mine."

I reached down and showed him my own belt. "A fine serrated cutting edge on the lower part of the back. Overnight, they may have been able to cut through their ropes."

"Or the terrorists found out what they were trying to do and took their belts away from them."

"It's a long shot. I know that. There's no way of knowing whether they could get the job done. Maybe they're secured by cables. Maybe they're handcuffed. They have no guns, and the boatmen have automatic rifles probably. Joe knows enough to bide his time until he's assured of success. And Julie, God knows if she could inch her way clinging to a cliff over five thousand feet of open space in the Grand Canyon, she won't be flappable here. Cool as a cucumber until time to act. Well, all I can say is, if they get loose, heaven help their enemies."

"You sound optimistic."

"I'm not."

The captain turned away. I went down to the deck, Apis trailing in my wake.

Lieutenant Applegate stood with binoculars, eyes fixed on the horizon.

"Is that the one?" he asked.

I handed the binoculars to Apis, who looked carefully, then nodded. I had no idea how he could tell. Perhaps it was merely because few feluccas come this far out, or at this early hour, or something...

I took out my phone and tried to call the Swains.

No response.

I tried again, with the same result.

The sun was rising a golden orange through the murk of the dusty Egyptian sky. The wind was calm, which led me to the assurance that the felucca had a motor on it. Otherwise, it could have made little headway with a heavy cargo.

I would have called Della except that it was well after midnight in Washington. Besides, she would have let me know if anything else had come up. She would have offered to get a restraining order from some admiral in Washington. I would not ask for it. I could have gone to the group admiral here in the Mediterranean.

No. It was not my idea to make an end-run around the captain. The logic of his position, no matter how many ways I might try to twist it, was inescapable. If the felucca was known to be loaded with explosives—which we ourselves had not examined and therefore had no first-hand proof—then the sailboat must be blown sky high.

We had only Apis's word. This whole affair could be the fabrication of a fertile, if twisted, imagination. I turned to him abruptly and asked again, with a vertical flat hand indicating the sailboat, and with spreading arms to signal BOOM! and pointed to the approaching felucca. Were there explosives aboard?

His head went up and down vigorously, and he swept his arms in an arc to indicate an explosion.

He was sure of it. I had no reason to doubt him. The matter was settled. To a terrorist, it must have represented a horrible logic and a daring devotion to Allah, all at the same time. And inescapable...

I asked Applegate: "What's the distance now?"

"Six kilometers and closing."

The statement had the ring of a death knell to it. "How fast?" I asked.

"Slowly," he answered. That was noncommital but I could tell that he had begun to get concerned. Then he added: "She has a heavy cargo."

He disappeared inside for a moment, and came back out with a headpiece containing a short antenna, mouthpiece and earphones. I noticed Apis watching with fascination as the lieutenant placed the contraption on his head, pulled out a cord, and fastened it to a small battery pack on his belt.

"Jed, do you read?" the lieutenant asked.

He listened for a moment. "Roger. Would you have Thurston get the helo ready?"

The request chilled my soul. Thurston, the helicopter pilot, would get ready to go out and send a rocket into the approaching time bomb.

FORTY TWO

The felucca had now come within visual range so that I could begin to distinguish objects on deck. The boat did seem to have a large cargo that bulged up in the center. The light was still not good enough, or the felucca close enough, to detect whether anyone was strapped to it. Two specks that moved about signified the boatmen, one on the bow, one at the stern.

That made it tough, Joe, I thought. *If you've cut your ropes and want to get these guys with your flying tackle, you can't do it. Not with one of them fore and the other aft. That would put Julie in danger. All you need is to start grappling with these guys over so many tons of explosive. Get them off balance. Send a bullet by accident into the cargo...and away you go. Joe, watch yourself.*

I didn't know how they were going to detonate the cargo, but at the moment that seemed like a useless question.

I felt certain that Joe was beginning to feel desperation. He and Julie must certainly know the intentions of the boatmen by now. The closer the boat and its cargo got to the carrier the more they could imagine the response of the captain. Without a shadow of a doubt, they were approaching sudden extinction.

I looked up at the bridge. The captain had come to the outer passageway and was looking down at us, watch-

ing everything that happened. I nodded to him and made a
motion of hopelessness. He matched it.

Below him, about two dozen sailors had come out on
an observation balcony called "Vulture's Row." How ironic,
I thought. When this was all over, there wouldn't be many
pieces to pick up.

I felt like a convicted criminal condemned to death,
waiting for the final order of execution.

Lieutenant Thurston came on deck and conferred
briefly with Lieutenant Applegate. I didn't hear what they
said. I didn't have to. Thurston would take off in his helicopter and hover a safe distance. That's all. Just stay there.
No hanging above this little boat. No trying to get close
and wave it off. If the presence of the military aircraft didn't
drive the felucca back, if the approach wasn't enough to
warn them away, then the pilot's action would be clear.

Arm a missile. Wait for command. Send it into the
felucca.

When they finished, Thurston left, walked aft to his
helicopter and climbed aboard. A deck maintenance man
went around the big machine, verifying to see that everything was go. An ordnance man checked the rockets strapped
beneath.

I put up the binoculars again and tried my best to
make out who else was in the felucca. Since it had drawn a
little closer, and the sun become a little brighter, I could
make out more of the cargo. At this point, I thought I could
see Julie and Joe strapped to it. Head and shoulders only.
Maybe it was my imagination.

*Joe, now would be a good time to begin your plan. If you
have one. If you intend to jump overboard, forget it. You'd be riddled
before you sank five feet. Make use of your flying tackle. Wait
until you get them together. Something. Anything. But you'd better be doing it pretty soon.*

"Five kilometers." The lieutenant said it without
emotion.

I looked up at the bridge. The captain had his binoculars focused on the approaching felucca.

Apis stood by the lieutenant, watching the operation with intense interest. He listened intently to the conversation between the lieutenant and the pilot. A conversation the little bull could not begin to grasp. But he could easily guess what they were saying and know what was about to happen.

I pointed my glasses back toward the felucca...and froze.

Two speedboats had come into view to the right of it, heading directly toward the sailboat.

It could only be some of the most hare-brained archeologists on the face of the earth. One look, and I knew that Tab and Veronica had been unable to sway them. I had no idea whether the pair had passed on to the rest of them my arguments, my orders. They may have. They may have done as I asked. But it only made the others more determined than ever to go.

The only thing clear was that they intended to carry out, stubbornly and dangerously, their plan to solve the whole situation.

The presence of two speedboats told me the worst. One would have held the four of them...Ali, Hami, Holly and Mei Hua...comfortably. Why the second boat?

I strained to fix my eyes on the second boat, beginning to get a sore spot on the nape of my neck. Surely it couldn't be what I was beginning to think it was. This has to be some kind of episode out of delirium tremens.

The more I looked, the more the images began to identify themselves. It was the Swains.

They had apparently parked their Land Rover, found the rest of the mob, and determined not to be left out themselves. When the others went to hire a boat, the Swains had hired one, too. I could just imagine them laughing with glee.

Now there were eight on our side about to die instead of two.

Sic semper gloria...

FORTY THREE

The speedboats slowed down to a crawl while still a hundred meters from the felucca. I could hear voices because sound travels well over water, but I couldn't detect any of the conversation.

Then came the sound of a couple of bursts from the automatic rifles, fired into the air. A warning by the boatmen.

That settled the issue of whether this was a terrorist vessel. Apis was now proved right. The captain should have no doubt. The lieutenant would have no doubt.

The purpose of the warning shots, I assumed, was to warn the speedboats to stay where they were. Or get out of the vicinity.

They didn't. They kept drifting closer.

I could now recognize the Swains in one boat, and Hami, Ali, Molly and Mei Hua in the other.

It struck me as incongruous that the normally meek and pensive Mei Hua could let herself get into such a hazardous situation. Her ancestors had engaged in lots of wars, but wars were still un-Chinese. Besides, I knew that the Chinese are nothing if not sincere, and if she perceived that she could help, even in a dangerous situation, nothing would keep her away.

And Molly, the schoolmarm. The seeker of logographic elements in Egyptian writing. How could she put herself into this?

Bravery resides in timid souls, is it not so? You, of all people know that, Barry Ross. Don't you remember Beryl and Dana in the Amazon? Surprised you, didn't they? And the Madam Professor Arden-Jones, oh what she did to the ILB boat that night on the Rio Ramón. Why should this be different? When touched with anger, you know the results. Might not one of these timid souls talk the gunmen out of it? Is that too simplistic for you to consider?

In a word, yes.

A figure stood up in the speedboat and shouted across the water. I presumed it to be Ali Fawzi, the only one among the lot who could converse with the boatmen. Or try to. I had no idea whether he was getting through to them or not.

He waved his arms and pointed to the carrier. The boatmen waved back, wildly, motioning both boats to get the hell out of there.

Nothing stopped Ali. The little guy who had been so downcast and disgruntled at Maybelle's my first night there was now a machine in perpetual motion. I would never have recognized him. I could not tell whether he was trying to negotiate for release of the captives, but whatever it was, he threw his heart, soul, voice, and waving arms into it.

His waving and jumping unsettled the boat, and he had to stoop to grasp the gunwale in order to steady himself and not fall overboard.

All the while, the speedboats drifted closer to the felucca. At that range, I knew, the boatmen could pick them off easily, one by one. Moreover, at that close range, the speedboats and their occupants would be absolutely wiped out if anything detonated the cargo.

My only hope was that none of them was foolish enough to bring a gun. Or issue any threats...

In this tinderbox, I would no longer be surprised, whatever happened. These ill-advised, foolhardy archeologists, untrained in the arts of war, had moved onto center stage, right in the middle of the battlefield, and become a crucial part of the fight. I could not tell whether Julie and Joe were trying to warn them away. I have no doubt that they were, but with no success. In such a babble of voices, reason seemed to be lost.

The boatmen shouted back, again motioning the speedboats away. I had no way of predicting when the terrorists would tire of this and spray the little boats with lead. If that happened—and no one could stop them—it would be too late to rescue them from this folly. I didn't see how rescue was humanly possible, anyway, but they were making failure a certainty.

The felucca kept on course for the carrier. The speedboats kept pace beside it.

Within moments the speedboats had closed to within ten meters of the sailboat. I could not imagine that they intended to board the felucca, but now it occurred to me that, foolish as they were in everything else, maybe they were going to try it. That would be the nadir of absurdity.

On the other hand, it was quite possible, though I tried not to think of it, that the boatmen had ordered them aboard.

A bonanza. Six more offerings to Allah.

If that were the case, I could only say to the Swains that I had warned them about this and did all I could to stop their whole nightmarish plan. If they got caught in the middle of this disaster, it was of their own making. Without any help whatsoever to Julie and Joe.

"Four kilometers," said Lieutenant Applegate.

Apis stood beside him. I gave the glasses to Apis so that he could see what was going on. He took one look, then glanced at me and shook his head vigorously. I spread my hands helplessly. There wasn't anything we could do about it. Applegate had the only viable plan, and he glanced back to Thurston and the helicopter.

"Initiate flight control," he said into his microphone. He gave the hand and arm signal to start the aircraft. In a few moments, the rotors began to turn.

FORTY FOUR

Apis handed the glasses back to me. With the felucca closer, I could now see much more clearly that Julie and Joe were indeed strapped to the cargo. They appeared to be doing nothing but watch the proceedings. I thought I heard Joe bellowing to the archeologists, but in the confusion I couldn't distinguish the words. Ali waved his hands and shouted. The Swains chorused some words in Arabic. Molly chimed in, along with Hami. It was a verbal free-for-all that could not last much longer.

I tried to figure out what Joe might do if indeed they had managed to untie their hands. The speedboats out there represented a complication. But there was one advantage. Ali and the others had diverted the attention of the boatmen, and that would be of some remote benefit. If only Joe could use it.

The time dragged excruciatingly on. It was like a slow-motion horse race in which you had to wait an eternity for your horse to win.

A few moments later, the shouting match seemed to end. Ali talked to the boatmen in calmer tones, with less flailing of the arms. I could still hear them, and the voices grew louder as the felucca came closer. But the rising noise of the helicopter on board began to drown everything out.

I glanced at the captain. He had his glasses trained on the cluster of boats. Then he turned toward the helicopter aft. Lieutenant Thurston soon hàd the rotors up to speed. The craft was almost ready.

Ali Fawzi still gestured from the front of the speedboat. The Swains waved their arms. All of this, I assumed, was an attempt to play on the sympathy of the boatmen. Pleas to save innocent lives. To think of mothers and children left behind. To remember that Allah was compassionate and merciful.

There was no way I could tell whether the boatmen even understood what they were trying to say.

I gave the rescuers zero chance of succeeding. Others had no doubt played on the sympathy of killers before, without success. I could imagine the boatmen trying to convince them, *Get out of our way so we can get this job done.*

That was their dedicated mission and no one, no matter how much they waved their arms and shouted, was going to talk them out of it.

I couldn't see why Ali had thought otherwise. He and the rest of them lived in the midst of periodic turmoil, most recently the bombing of Coptic churches in southern Egypt. Dozens of fatalities, and no way of explaining it except religious fervor against "infidels." Ali must have coped with this all his life. He was not stupid. What was I missing? How was I misinterpreting his zeal?

I looked back up at the captain, as though pleading for a miracle. He slowly shook his head. He knew what I knew. There were no miracles in the carrier's arsenal. No sudden relief. Only the relentless march toward death.

Apis grabbed my glasses to look again, but registered nothing more than another vigorous shake of the head.

Applegate turned aft, lifted his arms, and spoke into his tiny microphone. I could not hear what he said, but the aim was clear. The three-kilometer limit was about to be breached. The time had come.

Lieutenant Thurston lifted the chopper, flew out over the side of the carrier and headed for the felucca.

FORTY FIVE

Visibly agitated, Apis ran up to me, gesturing wildly. That helicopter is going to bomb that felucca?

I nodded sadly and made some motions of rockets zooming into the sailboat. He jumped around, approached Lieutenant Applegate with a stream of Arabic, pointing to the helicopter and felucca and gesturing wildly. The lieutenant gestured to him that the felucca was getting too close, and if it got too close it would go BOOM! (wide sweep of arms), and the carrier would disappear.

Apis put his arms in friendship around the lieutenant, still shaking his head, then backed off, muttering mournful words to himself.

In the loudest voice I could possibly manage, I shouted: "JOE! JOE! GET OUT OF THERE! NOW!"

That was rather stupid. There was no way my voice could have carried that far. But the chopper was downwind, and Julie and Joe had good ears. I thought it was worth a try.

Lieutenant Applegate watched and waited. Once he looked at me, sadly, and said: "I don't want to kill them any more than you do."

All my experiences with Joe—in the Amazon, down the Grand Canyon, in Wyoming, the wedding, everything—

flashed by in split-seconds. All the efforts expended in training him, the prospect of losing them both in a useless, silly blast, fell on my head like an anvil.

However, I knew that he must realize that it was getting very close to time to act. If they had both cut their bonds, they ought to be ready.

A sudden thought chilled me. Perhaps they had already tried to act and had been riddled by automatic rifle fire. Perhaps they had been propped up, dead and done with. Sent to Allah early.

I put the binoculars to my eyes and focused as sharply as I could. The helicopter was now hovering about a kilometer from the boats. The members of Maybelle's mob had become agitated, too, seeing the chopper so close. If ever it was to become clear to them what was about to happen, it was now.

Lying down in front of a bulldozer was one thing. Getting in front of a loaded felucca headed for a carrier was another.

Act, Joe! Act! Move out of there!

No movement. Nothing.

I waved my arms. If they were alive, perhaps they would see me and decide to move. Of course, it was always possible that they *couldn't* move, that they had been injured, their legs shot up, their arms shattered, or couldn't cut through thick ropes, or were immobilized by cables.

With wide swings, I motioned them to get off the boat, to get out of the way.

It didn't work. Nothing worked. Nothing happened.

The chopper waited for a signal from the lieutenant.

The lieutenant waited for a signal from the captain.

I looked up. The captain still had his glasses on the boats. Then he looked down at the lieutenant, and at me. He said nothing. He did not even move his head, or spread his hands in a gesture of despair. His moment of decision was getting very, very close.

I pleaded silently with the boatmen to give up, turn coward, put up a white flag, back off. I grabbed at the wildest straws, knowing nothing would work, that all must now be futile. They were determined to do what damage they could, and if they got blown up doing it, even that far from the carrier, they would still be heroes.

Everybody in the speedboats seemed to be gesturing and shouting. The boatmen climbed up on the edge of the felucca. I thought they must be getting ready to fire down into the boats, spray all the occupants with lead, and die even greater heroes.

No, that didn't seem their intention. The automatic rifles were still slung over their shoulders. They motioned the boats to back off. Motioned the mob to get down low. To escape while they could. To go. Go away. Now!

The moments of frustration and lack of any action began to freeze in my brain like a scene from some celestial ballet that had suddenly turned into slow motion. Nothing was happening, even on the eve of a horrendous Armageddon. This was the point in a nightmare where I usually waked in a pool of sweat. There was no waking now. But there was a lot of sweat. This was for real.

Everything seemed at a standstill, waiting the final moment.

I looked up. How long would the captain wait? The felucca was drifting closer. It was now *inside* the three kilometer range. If he didn't act within…

I stopped thinking about it. He looked down at me sadly, then looked toward Lieutenant Applegate…and nodded.

The lieutenant turned to me with as sad a face as I had ever seen, horrified at what he must do, knowing that there were Americans on that felucca and in those speedboats. Living, breathing Americans who were doing nothing more than trying to stop all this from happening.

They had been warned. The lieutenant had delayed enough already. He could delay no longer. He looked up at the captain again for corroboration. The captain nodded slowly.

Every sound seemed to stop in my ears, even the distant sound of the chopper. The only sound I was waiting for now was Applegate's signal, the death knell of Julie and Joe.

And then it came.

The lieutenant said into his microphone: *"Fire!"*

FORTY SIX

I turned my head. There was no way I could watch the fireworks. Watch Julie and Joe disappear in a blast of fire and smoke.

Julie and Joe and Tab and Veronica, Hami, Ali, Molly, and Mei Hua. All of them. Gone in a flash.

Closing my eyes, I waited.

The seconds passed like hours. Five seconds, ten, fifteen.

My eyes began to open slowly. I turned around.

Applegate was frowning. Nothing had happened.

I looked at Apis. He had turned toward me, smiling, suppressing a giggle, pointing toward the lieutenant's waist.

Then I saw what had happened, though the lieutenant was unaware of it.

When Apis had embraced the lieutenant, he had deftly pulled the microphone plug from the battery pack on Applegate's belt.

The lieutenant's order had not been transmitted.

I put up my glasses. Everything was as before.

But now I saw some movement *behind* the boatmen. Joe—I almost shouted with delight—it was Joe, rising and moving forward, slowly approaching the boatmen as they stood on the edge of the felucca, waving off the mob in the speedboats.

I shouted to the lieutenant. "Wait! Wait!"

Joe broke into full gallop and sailed toward the boatmen in a flying tackle, a masterful feat he had practiced on the gridiron.

They turned at the sound, but it was too late.

Joe sailed between them, arms outstretched. With a powerful force he took them both with him overboard and into the sea.

"He's got them overboard!" I shouted, though I knew that the lieutenant was also watching.

It was almost impossible to see what was happening in the splashing water. The speedboats drifted around and obscured part of the action.

Applegate shouted into his microphone. "Hold your fire!"

Apis and I knew that that order would not have gone out either. I walked up to him and took the dangling cord in my hand. "This came loose," I said.

He looked down in horror, plugged it in again and said: "Thurston, do you copy?"

The answer must have satisfied him. Then: "Hold your fire. The boatmen are off the felucca."

I watched Julie leap off the felucca and join the fray in the water.

It did not seem possible to me that the boatmen could last long against Julie and Joe. With a little luck, Joe could disarm them, hurl their automatic weapons away and let them sink in forty fathoms. I could not tell whether he was trying to rescue the boatmen, or leave them there to die with the felucca.

In any case, what followed was a frantic clambering aboard the speedboats. I could hear shouting and cheering. In moments, their voices were swallowed by the roar of the motors as the speedboats sped away in flying spray, as fast as they could go.

"Now!" Applegate shouted into the microphone. "*Fire!*"

This time I didn't mind watching. The relief that flooded over me within the space of a few seconds was greater than any I had ever experienced. Julie and Joe were free! So was the mob, all of them speeding out of harm's way.

Thurston waited another moment. Then the missile left the helicopter. Leaving a bright trail, it struck the felucca and detonated the cargo.

The mast came apart in splinters. The huge sail ripped and disappeared. Planks shot out in all directions in the midst of an enormous blast of fire and jets of gray smoke. The fire coalesced into a ball that expanded and rose amid the clutter of flying debris.

The heat struck my face, and the force of the blast swept by me like a gust of wind. Joyous, I looked up at the captain. He was smiling broadly, giving me a thumbs up gesture.

Fragments of debris fell into the ocean. The speedboats became visible through the smoke, heading for shore. Applegate said into the microphone: "Okay, return to deck."

He turned to me, wiping his forehead, and shook my hand with a powerful grip. "Man! I never want to come that close to killing our own people—ever again!"

Apis shook hands with him. "I have to confess to you, lieutenant, that we owe it all to Apis. Apis and Joe."

"What?"

"This is one crafty little guy. When he put his arms around you a while ago, he pulled the plug from your battery pack.

Applegate slapped his forehead, leaned back and roared. "So *that's* how it happened. I thought I must have been careless. Well, this little guy deserves a reward, and I am going to go get it for him."

He left, just as the captain came up and shook my hand.

"Barry, I would never have guessed," he said, "that this would have come out so well."

"Oh," I said, adopting a nonchalant stance, "my assistants have perfect timing. Besides, that little Apis pulled the plug from Applegate's battery pack and the order to fire never got out."

As the captain roared with laughter, the lieutenant came up with a twelve-inch model of the carrier, planes and all, and handed it to the little bull.

Apis beamed and threw his arms around the lieutenant. This time, though, he took care not to pull the plug.

FORTY SEVEN

By the time we got to Maybelle's that evening, the crowd was so exuberant that I thought they would surely drain her supply of liquid refreshments. Junji had made up, on short notice, a fresh batch of chicken shumais. They went so fast, in this starving crowd, that he had to scurry back to the kitchen to make some more.

I looked around for Sandy Santano, but Maybelle said he and Dr. Gholub were out at the tombs making a complete numerical and visual catalog of the contents. Biggest find in years, Maybelle said, gushing. "It was Turki's legacy to us. Everybody here likes him now."

"Yeah," I said, "now that he's dead."

She gave me a hug and said: "Barry, you have done a wonderful job. You'll never know how grateful we all are."

"Little Apis did a wonderful job," I said. "And Julie and Joe remembered their training very well."

The Swains burst upon us, arguing, as usual, but not as vehemently because they had so much to celebrate.

"You almost screwed the whole thing up," I said, tongue in cheek.

Tab responded: "It was all her fault..."

I got out of there fast.

Hami exulted because he had talked with Dr. Gholub, who promised to be more communicative and helpful than Turki had been. Ali Fawzi had been assigned to continue looking for more ancient Egyptian roads, and tonight he beamed.

Molly asked me when we were going to get together for some more discussion about the logographic elements of Egyptian writing, and I answered: "On the plane to Singapore."

"I'm not going to Singapore," she said, surprised.

"Well, then, Molly, it will have to be some other time. I leave just before midnight."

"You just got here!" she said, in the understatement of the night.

I embraced Mei Hua, and there wasn't much we could say. I told her in Chinese that I thought she was one of the bravest persons I had ever known.

"Not so!" she said. "Bu shi! Bu shi! Not at all." That's the Chinese way of responding to praise. I shook her hand and said "Zai jian, zai jian." Till we meet again. The Chinese never say goodbye.

Maybelle saw me to the door. "I shall write to Kelly," she said, "to tell her how brilliant and brave you were."

"Don't you dare!" I responded. "With her I don't need any more praise."

"I'll do it in the hopes she'll send you back."

"Maybelle, you're sweet. You must keep up your good work here. There'll never come an end to the good that you are doing."

I bade them all goodbye and went out to my car.

FORTY EIGHT

I had one more task before leaving Egypt. There was one other person I had to say goodbye to.

Ten minutes later, I inserted my key into the apartment door and stepped inside.

She was standing in the doorway to her kitchen, clad in the same translucent gown she wore the last time I came. On the table burned the usual candle and there, too, was a new vase with a carnation in it.

She glared at me with her deep black eyes, the same rockets glaring, and I could tell at a glance that she had not forgiven me for my last abbreviated visit.

"Hello, Andrea," I said. "I hope you're not still mad at me."

She said nothing, but scowled and glided swiftly over to the flower vase. Picking it up, she made to throw it at me when I caught her hand.

"You have forgotten," I said softly. "The Spanish are some of the most forgiving people on earth."

"No, they're *not!*" she said, trying to wrest the vase from me.

I held fast, and in a few moments she yielded. Not to give up, I knew, but to try a new tack.

"I just came to say goodbye," I said, softly. "Am I not polite and considerate?"

She looked away. I set the vase on the floor beneath the table where it would not be so immediately accessible, then pointed to the balcony. "Aren't you going to invite me out for one last look at Cairo?"

Clearly, she wanted to hurl me from the balcony, but she did as I suggested, without smiling.

Out there, the evening breeze lifted the chiffon gown and revealed the glistening oils on her thigh.

As we stood beside each other, gazing out over the lights and the river, I said: "I wanted to thank you again for getting me such a wonderful room in the hotel. Only you knew where I was staying and only you could have had the cobra put there. Do you remember that?"

She stiffened, and a faint trace of sudden fear crossed her face.

"Only you could have sent that sniper to try to nail me as I jogged near the hotel."

The fear, the shock, the terror in her face turned her countenance into an impassive mask.

"Turki Husseini," I went on, "was a very lucky man, wasn't he? You had him here many times. He enjoyed your hospitality so much that he would let you in on his deepest secrets from time to time. He trusted you because you were in Maybelle's employ. Isn't that right?"

She glowered and said nothing.

"And on that last night... Oh that was the most exciting of all, wasn't it? You got him drunk. He gave you a map to the new tombs, just the thing your syndicate was trying so hard to find."

She hauled off and tried to slap me square across the face, but I caught her wrist and pulled it behind her back. Pulling the other hand around behind, despite her kicking and growling, I lashed them together with a section of plastic handcuff cord.

She struggled for a while, then ceased.

"And then," I continued, "you erased the evidence with a little stiletto. It took Samaan and me quite a while to find the little hole. Andrea, I have to admire you. You have leadership qualities. Who else could have held together such a crowd of goons as Zebec and his colleagues? I suppose they all had keys, too..."

She struggled to free herself and, failing that, gave me a solid kick on the shins.

"Now, now," I said, "calm down. I think I knew all along that you were Isis, because Isis was the goddess of fertility. I liked that. It was a nice alias. I mean, wife of Osiris, mother of Horus... You were *somebody*. You commanded a lot of respect among the Egyptians, even though few in the syndicate knew who Isis was. Very nice going."

She let her head drop in dejection.

"Except for one," I went on. "One little faceless Egyptian. Little Apis brought your empire down because he was proud of Egypt, and he didn't want to see anyone taking away its treasures. This country needs more Apises, don't you think...?"

At this, she spat on me, and I terminated the conversation.

The door opened.

Omar Samaan had arrived as I requested, just in time. His security men swarmed into the apartment and took over, getting out a robe to clothe Andrea.

Omar shook my hand vigorously and said, "How can we repay you enough for what you have done for Egypt?"

I responded: "You know little Apis?"

"Yes."

"He did a lot for Egypt. The Swains will tell you all about it."

"Yes, sir. Then we will respect him. We will give him a medal."

"Could you also give him a good job, Omar?"

"Promise, Barry, promise. Now would you like to go to a show?"

"Oh, I do wish I could, Omar. I remember the last one so well. But my plane leaves tonight. I have to go to Australia."

"Good belly dancers. Maybe you wait another night?"

"Next time, Omar. I promise."

Behind him, Julie and Joe came into view.

Joe looked around, saw the robed prisoner, and turned to me like a scolding mother. "Barry! What is the meaning of this?"

"Meaning of what?"

"She's almost naked. What have you been up to? Aren't you ashamed?"

"Why?" I asked. "She's a beautiful woman, is she not? Would you be ashamed?"

Julie answered quickly: "Yes, he would! Well, I don't think she's so beautiful with those handcuffs. What's going on?"

I ushered them into the hall, saying: "I'll tell you on the way to the airport."

As we got into the car and sped across Cairo, Joe relaxed and said: "Boy is it going to feel good to relax around that pool for a week."

I burst his bubble. "God knows we're grateful for what you did, both of you. But our plane leaves for Singapore in three hours, and we have to stop by Club Med to get your luggage."

He sat upright. "What are you saying?"

"I'll tell you on the way to Singapore."

Julie turned to me with a frown. "Now wait a minute. Barry, I have got to put my foot down. What about our honeymoon?"

"Surprise," I said. "How would you like a honeymoon on Dinkum Island?"

"We will not be put off again. This is it."

She paused and looked at me with those inquisitive eyes. "Where," she asked, "is Dinkum Island?"

▶▶▶

Colophon

The text of *The Isis Command* is set in 11.5 point Garamond3 on 12.5 point leading. Introductory pages and chapter titles are in the RotisSemiSerif and Post Antigua families. Special characters are derived from Pompeijana Borders and various images styled after ancient Egyptian art elements.

The text stock is 60 lb Eureka Recycled Opaque. It is acid-free for archival durability, and it meets or exceeds all guidelines set forth by the U. S. Environmental Protection Agency for recycled content and use for post-consumer waste. The binding is Perfect Bind.

The printer is Commercial Documentation Services, Medford, Oregon 97501 (Doug Casey, Account Manager).

The cover, text and special character design and production are by Dan Schiffer, Digimedia, Jacksonville, Oregon 97530. All cover images are derived from copyrighted photographs of the author.

The book was produced on an Apple Power Macintosh 8500 using PageMaker 6.5.

Trademarks: Apple and Macintosh are registered trademarks of Apple Computer, Inc. PageMaker is a registered trademark of Adobe Systems, Inc.

The following is an excerpt from Ann Livesay's
forthcoming

DEATH IN THE AMAZON
A Barry Ross International Mystery

*{Barry Ross has come to the Colombian Amazon to deliver a
fiery speech about preserving tropical forests or risk world ecologi-
cal disaster... After the meeting he joins ten others on a dugout
canoe trip down the Orteguasa River to relax and spend a week
with the Correguaje Indians. One member of the group infuriates
the other passengers, and is soon found dead. Thugs from his land-
buying company in Bogotá harass the group to find who did it...and
Barry harasses the thugs back. In the midst of all this, Palkuh
Mamha-uh, the old chief of a village taken over by gold miners is
kidnaped. Every member of the group insists on going up the Rio
Ramón at night to rescue him. They are led by Aunamunh, the
nearly-a-teenager, who knows the way by heart. After a harrow-
ing nighttime paddle, they arrive at the primitive village dock.
While the rest wait upstream at the river's edge, Aunamunh leads
Barry and Joe toward the village, tells them to stop, then goes on
in alone. They wait in the silence...and wait...and wait... As
Barry tells the story...}*

Two figures, one medium height, one small, approached in the pitch blackness to within arm's length.
Aunamunh led the Red Chief to us. The Chief limped. He
had been hurt. He threw his arms around Joe, then me.
Not a word passed among us.

Joe handed his rifle to me and bent down so that the
old chief could grasp his shoulders and climb up on his
back. Then, holding a slender tree trunk for leverage, Joe
pulled himself and his burden up. Without delay, we started
our slow, silent trek back toward the river.

As slowly and as maddeningly as we had come from
it. Palkuh would seem to grow heavier with each step. Joe's
arms must be growing numb. He swayed under the heavy

load and uncertain footing, trying to avoid the spiny tree trunks... And the stringy spider webs with their fist-sized denizens.

No sound came from behind. No light either. So far, so good. The miners in the village were still asleep, guns at their sides.

We reached the miners' speed boat at the edge of the river. Joe set Palkuh down. I took the chief's arm and we walked upstream to join the others.

Every passenger expressed jubilation in near silence. Joe carried the chief to one of the canoes and set him in it. We all got aboard as quietly as we could and picked up the oars.

Suddenly a sound of gunfire came through the forest. Light beams from powerful flashlights jabbed among the trees.

I shouted: "They found us! Get out of here!"

We plunged our paddles into the water, caution gone.

"Pull, everybody!" Joe shouted with the full force of his lungs. "We don't have much time!"

They didn't need urging. Each passenger pulled for his life. We could barely see the wall of trees on the other side of the Rio Ramón, and headed there, straining to get as far away from the dock as we could before the miners arrived.

The lights became brighter, the sounds closer. Shouts rang out, muffled by the mists, absorbed in the dense tropical forest.

We moved with excruciating slowness out beyond the speedboat, headed downstream.

Miners burst out of the trees and ran down the embankment to the edge of the water. Their lights found the intruders. Their guns took aim.

"Stay down!" I shouted, knowing that no one could row and stay down at the same time. "Keep as low as you can!"

Bullets zinged across the water, whacked into the canoes and severed twigs overhead.

Greg Fisher lurched against the side of the canoe. Beryl cried out.

"I'm okay," he said, "top of the shoulder."

Beams of light converged on us as we paddled in desperation. Lights blinded us after so long in the darkness. Bullets struck the water, whined past, pinged above our heads.

Then, ominously, the miners began to clamber into the speedboat.

Moments later we swerved around the bend, out of sight of the miners.

Their guns still fired, though blindly now. The captives had been taken from them, and their rage knew no bounds.

I got out my 9mm Parabellum pistol and laid it beside me in the canoe. "Keep paddling," I ordered. "They'll catch up to us any moment."

The shooting stopped. We could still hear rapid-fire shouts and curses, Latin style. Above the clatter of our paddling, I could hear the miners starting up. The engine burst into life with a rumble. The boatman gunned it.

I had a vivid imagination. I knew what was happening. I could see the miners picking up grenades as the boat jumped out of the water and headed downstream toward us.

The others heard it, too. We pulled with all our might.

My heart sank as I heard the loud whine of the speedboat coming closer, but still not visible.

You sure as hell got yourself and a dozen others in a pickle this time, my alter ego chided me. How can you guys, with pissant paddles, get out of the way of a speedboat with armed miners coming at you mad as hell? Answer that one, smart boy.

I had no answer. We could break away and head into the deep forest, but there wasn't any time for that. We'd have to fight. And the miners held all the upper hands.

With a burst of lights and a deafening roar, the speedboat rounded the bend and came into view. We recoiled, blinded.

The miners instantly spotted us. Snapping their automatics to their shoulders, they took aim...

"This is it," I said to myself, raising my pistol.

Weirdly, my thoughts flew back to New York City. I almost spoke aloud, as if addressing someone far away: "Kelly, I hope to hell you see what you got us into this time...?"

About the Author

Ann Livesay is that rare combination of geologist, author, and scientific researcher who takes readers where few other writers have gone—deep into dangerous places worldwide. She has worked in these places, photographed them, and written about them in 22 nonfiction books coauthored with her husband, Myron Sutton. In the Barry Ross International Mysteries, she brings her skills directly to readers, with authenticity of locale guaranteed. She takes you in, with bold and daring suspense, and knows how to get you back out... Maybe.

To order more copies of *The Isis Command*, send check or money order for $US12.95 per copy, postpaid, or send Visa or Mastercard number with Expiration Date, to Silver River, Inc., 1619 Meadowview Drive, Medford, OR 97504. Or visit our Web site at http://www.silverriver.com. If you would like to be notified when more volumes in the Barry Ross International Mysteries appear, please write to Silver River and you will be put on the mailing list.